Their gazes connected.

A bond that had formed from the very beginning strengthened, and Madison started to envision more. She saw the possibility in his look and could even tell the exact moment he realized there was something beyond the case that was going on between them. His eyes blazed, and his intense regard took in her features as though he were reassessing his thoughts about them.

He pulled her into his embrace and just held her against him. "*Thank you* isn't adequate for what I feel."

His aftershave teased her senses. The feel of his arms sent a wave of contentment through her. What was happening to her? Surely these feelings were because of their heightened emotions concerning the case. She did not want to be hurt again. She did not want to mistake this for something it wasn't.

Books by Margaret Daley

Love Inspired Suspense

Hearts on the Line #23
Heart of the Amazon #37
Vanished #51

Love Inspired

The Power of Love #168
Family for Keeps #183
Sadie's Hero #191
The Courage to Dream #205
What the Heart Knows #236
A Family for Tory #245
Gold in the Fire #273
A Mother for Cindy #283

Light in the Storm #297
The Cinderella Plan #320
When Dreams Come True #339
Tidings of Joy #369

*The Ladies of Sweetwater Lake

MARGARET DALEY

feels she has been blessed. She has been married more than thirty years to her husband, Mike, whom she met in college. He is a terrific support and her best friend. They have one son, Shaun. Margaret has been writing for many years and loves to tell a story. When she was a little girl, she would play with her dolls and make up stories about their lives—now she writes these stories down. She especially enjoys weaving stories about families and how faith in God can sustain a person when things get tough. When she isn't writing, she is fortunate to be a teacher for students with special needs. Margaret has taught for over twenty years and loves working with her students. She has also been a Special Olympics coach and participated in many sports with her students.

VANISHED

Margaret Daley

Steeple
Hill®

Published by Steeple Hill Books™

STEEPLE HILL BOOKS

Steeple
Hill®

ISBN-13: 978-0-373-44241-6
ISBN-10:   0-373-44241-6

VANISHED

Faith is the substance of things hoped for,
the evidence of things not seen.
                    —*Hebrews* 11:1

To the Steeple Hill editors
You all are the best

ONE

"Go away!" Sitting on the navy-and-beige couch, Kim switched the cordless phone to the other ear and turned from her little sister to face the bookcases along one wall in the den.

"But you said you would help me." Ashley stamped her foot. "I have to have it done by tomorrow."

"Just a minute, Lexie." Kim cupped the receiver, glared over her shoulder at Ashley and blew a bubble, the pop of the gum loud. "Can't you see I'm busy. I'll help you later. Go outside and play."

"But—"

"I'll let you know when I'm ready to help." Kim infused into her voice all the frustration she was experiencing at her little sister's constant bugging. When Ashley didn't budge from the spot where she'd planted herself five minutes ago, Kim firmed her mouth into a frown she hoped conveyed all her feelings. "Go! Now, brat!"

"I'm telling Daddy when he comes home you've been on the phone for over an hour."

The whine hovered in the air between the two sisters.

Kim narrowed her eyes. With a glare, Ashley spun around and stormed out of the den.

The slamming of the back door echoed through the house. Kim pried her hand loose from over the receiver and put it to her ear as she pushed herself off the couch and walked to the bay window to make sure Ashley stayed in the backyard. "She's gone. I don't understand why I always get stuck babysitting. My brother should have to some of the time."

"At least your dad pays you. My mom doesn't." Her best friend's pout could be heard through the phone.

The fact she got paid didn't appease Kim at the moment. Having an eight-year-old always following her around made her wish she didn't have a little sister.

The watcher spied the little blond girl stalk out of the house. The sound of the door slamming against its frame drowned out the dog's barking a few houses down for a couple of blissful seconds.

I'll return later to take care of that dog, but right now I've got more important concerns. Anticipation surged. *His* daughter, so close the watcher's palms itched.

The child made a beeline for the swing set and plopped down on the seat, grabbing hold of the chains to keep herself upright.

The little girl's mouth moved. The watcher strained to hear what she was saying, but her voice was pitched too low.

No matter. After years of planning it wouldn't change what had to be done.

J. T. Logan will regret his very existence by the time

I'm through toying with him. Everything's in place for the merry ride he's about to go on.

"Ashley. Kim," J.T. yelled when he stepped through the front door of his house.

Ashley was usually waiting for him to tell him the latest Kim transgression against her. Ever since his oldest daughter had turned fourteen, all the sisters did was fight. It had gotten to the point he was checking into day care for his youngest after school until he could get home from work. Being a single parent wasn't easy. He wished he had family he could turn to for help.

Maybe today they actually got along for a change. He'd certainly prayed to the Lord enough in the past months concerning his two daughters. God was probably getting tired of hearing from him, J.T. thought with a chuckle.

After the *long* day he'd put in at the sheriff's office, trying to pacify people who didn't want to be pacified, all he wished for was a warm dinner and a little peace. He cocked his head, realizing the place was too quiet. His youngest was so full of energy that she usually kept going strong right up to bedtime.

J.T. walked toward the den at the back of the house. Halfway down the hallway he heard Kim mumbling something he couldn't make out. When he entered the den, his oldest daughter quickly put the receiver in its cradle and bolted to her feet as though he hadn't seen her talking on the phone.

Ever since Kim had become a teenager, the phone wasn't far from her reach. Even setting limits on her phone time didn't stop her from spending half of her waking hours gabbing to her friends—not her family. It had never been that way with his son. But girls were different. "Where's your sister?"

Kim waved her hand toward the window. "Out back playing."

"Go get her. You two can help me make something for dinner. Neil will be home from baseball practice in an hour."

"Why don't we order pizza?"

"Because we had it two nights ago." J.T. left the den and headed for the kitchen to see what was in the refrigerator while his daughter hopefully obeyed and got Ashley.

His shoulders aching, he stood before the near-empty shelves, the cold air cooling him, and wondered how he was going to pull off dinner with the few items he had. Ketchup. Milk. Three eggs. Several cheese slices. An onion that had black spots on it. A few stalks of limp celery. He would have to go to the grocery store on the way home from the station tomorrow. Being short-handed at the sheriff's office because one of his deputies was on vacation was certainly takinig a toll on him.

Kim shuffled her feet across the tile floor and opened the back door. "Ashley!" A long pause, then his oldest daughter stepped out onto the patio, the screen door banging closed behind her, and shouted, "Ashley, you'd better get inside. Now!"

The exasperation in Kim's voice made J.T. lift his head and turn toward the back patio. By the tone of Kim's voice, he would be refereeing yet another fight this evening.

"Ashley, you're in *big* trouble. Get in here!"

Great! His oldest daughter had alerted the whole neighborhood. He walked out onto the patio. "Kim?"

She peered over her shoulder at him, all the exasperation in her voice showing clearly on her face. "She's mad at me. She's hiding."

"Why is Ashley mad at you?" He positioned himself next to Kim and began to scan the backyard.

"I wouldn't help her with her wildflower project when she wanted."

"In other words, you were talking on the phone and didn't have time for Ashley. I pay you—" J.T.'s words suddenly caught in his throat when he spotted one of his daughter's black patent leather shoes on the ground by the swing set. She'd begged him to buy them and for the past two weeks they had been on her feet constantly except when she'd gone to bed. So why was only one there?

Every cop instinct in him rose to the surface, reviving for a brief moment the dark years he'd spent in Chicago as a homicide detective. There he saw a side of life most people never saw. He forced down the panic that for just an instant surged through him. She was hiding, as Kim said, probably in her fort by the trees. Or she'd gone over to a friend's without permission.

The father in him believed that.

The sheriff in him didn't.

He'd been trained to expect the worst. J.T. hurried toward the swing set, his gaze making a sweep of the large backyard. He noted a couple of places to check to see if Ashley was hiding from her sister. But it wasn't like her to continue to hide when he came out. She liked to complain too much to him about Kim's transgressions against her.

He skirted the swing set and jogged toward the stand of trees and several large bushes along the back of his property near the chain-link fence. "Call some of her friends and see if she's there." When Kim didn't move, he added in a stern voice, "Now, Kim."

I need to know that Ashley is okay. That I'm letting my cop imagination get the better of me.

Heart pounding, J.T. inspected the area behind the grouping of pines and various types of bushes where Ashley often played with her friends or by herself. The downpour earlier that day would have washed away all footprints except recent ones. His gaze fixated on a lone pair of prints in the mud near the thickest brush. Cowboy boots, size nine or ten, worn by a person around a hundred and eighty pounds.

Someone came into his yard recently.

That thought renewed the earlier panic he was trying to suppress. For what purpose? To read the gas meter? He glanced toward it, twenty feet away and on the other side of the yard, and realized that wasn't a likely explanation.

Which in his mind left all the bad reasons someone would trespass on his property. *To do harm.* Again the panic rushed to the foreground. He worked to keep it under control. It wouldn't do him any good in a time of crisis.

He looked at the bushes that his youngest loved to play in. Her secret hiding place, she had told him once. "Ashley, it's time to come out!" The strength in his voice conveyed all the rising doubts that she wasn't hiding in her fort. But he had to check and hope for the best.

Although there was no sign of her footprints nearby, J.T. got down on his hands and knees, making sure not to disturb the area around the ones made by the cowboy boots, and crawled into a hole in the vegetation that Ashley used as a door to her fort. Mud oozed up between his fingers. The bottom part of his tan uniform pants was soaked almost instantly. Something dripped down onto his head from above. He peered up and another raindrop spattered his forehead.

Lord, let her be inside and just playing a prank on her sister and me. Please.

He parted some branches to reveal a cleared area where his daughter had left some of her toys. But that was all there was under the large group of bushes. He backed his way out, trying desperately to keep his professional calm about him.

This just means she's at a friend's house.

But as he stood, his gaze again caught sight of the two footprints of an adult who'd had a perfect view of his whole backyard from this vantage point. In his professional estimation there was only one reason someone would have been watching his house. That person had to be up to no good. In his line of work he had angered some hardened criminals who would love nothing better than to get back at him, who had in fact threatened that very thing.

And as an officer of the law, he'd been taught to assume the worst-case scenario with a missing child. It was always better to be safe than sorry. That thought sent J.T. racing for his back door. Visions of the missing children he had been involved with as a Chicago police officer flew across the screen in his mind.

Inside, Kim hung up and turned toward him. "She isn't at any of her friends'." Her gaze widened at the sight of him muddy and wet.

"Who did you call?"

As his daughter ticked off the long list of Ashley's friends, he ran his fingers through his damp hair. "Did anyone know where she might be?"

Tears welled in Kim's eyes as she shook her head. "Dad, where's Ashley?" A lone track coursed down her cheek. "I know we got into a fight, but why would she run away?"

Lord, I hope it's only that. J.T. couldn't believe he had thought that, but if she were missing and she hadn't run away, the alternative would be that she had been taken. And that chilled him to the bone. In Chicago some of those missing children cases he'd been involved in hadn't ended—

Reminded of the ugliness in life he'd left behind, J.T. snatched up the phone and called the station. Time was of the essence, especially if she had been kidnapped. Twisting away from Kim to cover the trembling in his hand that held the receiver, he counted the rings.

On the fourth one, his secretary and receptionist Susan Winn finally answered. "Mercer County Sheriff's Office. How may I help you?"

"J.T. here. Ashley's missing. Send a couple of deputies to my house."

"Missing? What happened?" Susan asked.

"I don't know. She isn't in our backyard where she was supposed to be and none of her friends know where she is. It isn't like Ashley to leave without letting someone know where she's going." Ashley was his child who always followed the rules.

"Do you want to put out an *Amber* Alert?"

The waver in Susan's voice as she asked about the alert forced J.T. to dig deep for the mantle of professionalism he wore in cases like this. But his secretary's question underscored the situation. He couldn't afford to fall apart—not with his daughter's life at stake.

"I'll call you back in a few minutes and let you know. I want to check with the neighbors first." *Please, God, let her be at one of their houses.*

"J.T., I—"

He lowered his voice so Kim wouldn't hear. "She's okay. She's probably next door or across the street. Got to go." *Dear Lord, I hope that is all it is.*

When he hung up, his hand lingered on the receiver for a few seconds as he composed himself for Kim. His heartbeat thundered in his ears. He drew in a deep, fortifying breath. He'd been involved in many cases where nothing had been wrong.

But the few—

He shook the thought from his mind and pivoted toward Kim. "I'm going to check with the neighbors. You need to stay right here and wait for my deputies. Don't open the door to anyone else. Understand?"

With tears still streaming down her face, Kim nodded. "Daddy, I didn't want…"

Hearing her call him Daddy tore at his fragile composure. She'd stopped using it several years ago when she'd informed him she was too big to call him Daddy. He pulled her to him for a quick hug. "Everything will be all right, honey." When he opened the back door, he said, "See if you can get hold of Neil at the baseball complex and have him come home."

"Hey, maybe Ashley went to see Neil practice." She grabbed the phone.

"Maybe. If so, I'll be next door. Lock the door after I leave."

He waited on the patio to hear the lock click into place. J.T. hated to quench Kim's theory. But Ashley disliked anything to do with sports and didn't even like to go to her brother's baseball games. So Ashley going there didn't seem likely.

At a jog he headed toward his nearest neighbor whose view of his backyard was blocked by his six-foot wooden fence down both sides of his yard that the previous owner had erected because he had wanted some privacy. That very privacy could have made it easier for someone to come onto his property undetected.

Day one, 9:30 p.m.: Ashley missing three hours

"Kim won't come out. She refuses to eat." Susan grabbed the pot of coffee and began to refill everyone's cups as distant thunder rumbled.

Exhausted, J.T. pushed himself to his feet, his muscles protesting the movement after the hour spent sitting at his kitchen table mapping out a strategy to find Ashley. "I'll talk to her."

The blaring of the phone cut into the silence. Its sound jarred J.T. He whirled around, reached across the glass table and grabbed the receiver before it rang again. "J.T. here."

"Sir, we checked all the places you gave us and found nothing," Deputy Derek Nelson said, frustration marking each word spoken.

All energy drained from J.T. His eyes squeezed shut for a second as he leaned against the table for support. "Go back over every square inch a second time. The church. The school. The park."

"Yes, sir."

J.T. slammed the phone down. "Derek reported nothing."

"We still have four more teams who haven't called in yet." Kirk Carver studied the map of the town and the surrounding countryside. "Maybe she wandered off and lost track of time and they'll find her."

Lost track of time? Three hours? After dark? J.T. faced his deputy and wanted to laugh. He knew in his gut that Ashley hadn't walked away from the yard willingly. Someone had taken her. What little evidence they had pointed in that direction. He needed to be searching like his sons. "As soon as I talk with Kim, I'm going back out. All this planning isn't doing my daughter any good."

"We need to coordinate where people look. We need—"

"I don't. You can," J.T. interrupted his deputy. "There's got to be something—some kind of evidence that will tell us what happened, where to look."

"We scoured your backyard before it got dark. Except for her shoe there was nothing."

"And those footprints by the bushes."

"We've taken a casting. There's still a possibility—"

"What possibility? That Ashley is at a friend's playing? That someone opened my back gate and innocently wandered into my yard to stand by the bushes and face the back of my house?" All his anger and frustration—held at bay while he'd focused on planning—swamped him. "Nothing about this feels like a missing person. No one has wanted to say it, but I think Ashley has been kidnapped."

Susan gasped, bringing her hand up to her mouth. "Why?"

J.T. swung his gaze toward his secretary. "If I knew that, I might know who."

"Are you sure?" Her eyes wide, she dropped her arm limply to her side.

"Don't you think with practically the whole town out looking for the past couple of hours we'd have found Ashley by now?"

"Sir, we still need—" Kirk paused a few seconds "—to drag the lake and search the surrounding woods. Your house isn't too far from it. The two teams checking all the places around the lake haven't reported in yet."

His deputy's statement hung heavy in the sudden silence. J.T. lowered his gaze to the tile floor, his hands clenching at his sides. "I know we'll have to drag the lake if she isn't found soon," he finally managed to say, though his throat closed around each word.

"She could have gone to the lake. Had an accident." Kirk downed the last of his coffee and stood.

J.T. didn't know which was worse: thinking Ashley was at the bottom of the lake or she was kidnapped. At least if she had been taken there was a possibility she was still alive. *Is that why I'm insisting she's been kidnapped?*

No, he knew the reason. The evil he had encountered in Chicago nearly destroyed him to the point he had tried to forget the ugliness by drinking. Now he felt in his gut his past had come back to haunt him.

"We'll do it first thing tomorrow morning if we haven't found her by then." J.T. scanned his kitchen. "And we need to move the command post down to the station."

"J.T.," Rachel Altom, another one of his deputies, said from the doorway, "I've cataloged everything in Ashley's room and secured it. You need to go through it and determine if anything is missing."

Only an hour ago he'd briefly checked Ashley's room to see if her favorite doll or stuffed bear was missing. Both had been on her bed in their usual place, mocking him with their presence. The rest of his survey of his daughter's belongings had been quick. He'd barely held himself together and didn't know how he was going to do a more thorough search.

"I didn't see anything earlier, but I'll do it again." J.T. didn't say it was a waste of time. He knew in his heart his daughter hadn't run away, but this investigation needed to be by the book and he was the only one who could do the search.

"I need to talk to Kim again." Rachel took a mug of coffee that Susan handed her. "Now that she's had time to think, I want to make sure she's positive about what Ashley was wearing."

J.T. shook his head. "I'll do it. But unless Ashley changed after school, what Kim told you was right." He remembered his oldest daughter fleeing to her room an hour ago, refusing to talk to anyone. The longer Ashley was gone the more silent Kim had become.

J.T. plodded across the kitchen and passed Rachel at the doorway. The hallway to the bedrooms lay before him. The sight of Kim's and Ashley's closed doors tightened his chest, making breathing difficult. As he approached Kim's room, he drew in one shallow breath after another but nothing alleviated the pressure. It felt as if his heart had broken into hundreds of pieces.

For the first time in years, since his time in Chicago, he wanted a drink. He wanted to drown his pain in a bottle of alcohol, to forget that evil existed. His hand shook as he reached for the handle.

Lord, I can't go back to that kind of life. Help me! Bring Ashley home safely.

He knocked softly on Kim's door, then pushed it open. Kim sat trancelike in front of her small TV set, listening to the Amber Alert broadcasted over the Central City television station. He moved closer as his daughter rewound the tape and began to play it again. He touched her shoulder and leaned forward to switch off the TV.

"Kim—"

"Daddy, I'm sorry. I'm so sorry." She spun toward him and threw her arms around his waist.

Although she buried her face against him, he heard her sobs and the tightness in his chest expanded. Stroking her hair, J.T. fought to keep his own tears under control. For the past few hours they were ever present, a huge lump in his throat.

He swallowed several times. "Honey, you're *not* at fault." He managed to kneel next to her and cup her face, forcing his daughter to look at him. "Do you hear me? You didn't do anything wrong."

"You paid me to look after her, not talk on the phone. I told her to go out back and play. If she hadn't, she would—"

He pressed his fingers over her lips. "Shh. Ashley played out back all the time, often by herself. You had no idea this would happen to her." He regretted his admonition of Kim earlier, but there was no way he could take it back. His words uttered in frustration would be with both of them for a long time. He knew what guilt could do to a person. He'd dealt with it six years ago with his drinking and his wife's death.

"What if she ran away because of me?"

If only that was the extent of it. Another deep breath to fill his oxygen deprived lungs and J.T. said, "Let's not play what-ifs. It won't help Ashley, and it won't help you. Now, I need you to go over one more time what Ashley was wearing when she went outside to play."

She closed her eyes, a tear leaking out. "I told Rachel what she was wearing."

"Tell me again." He pushed her bangs from her eyes. He hated adding to Kim's pain by interrogating her. But it had to be done.

"She had on her blue jeans with the butterflies around the hem and her pale pink T-shirt and no jacket because it was warm." Kim came to a shaky stop, blinking rapidly. "Do you think she's cold? It still gets cold at night in May, Daddy."

He ignored her question because he didn't have a good answer. Instead he asked, "Which pair of shoes was she wearing?"

"Her black patent leather ones. That's all she wears anymore. I caught her one night sleeping—" Kim brought her hand up to cover her mouth and her tears returned to flow down her cheeks. "But now she's missing one," she mumbled through her fingers.

He couldn't hold his own sorrow back any longer. His tears left a wet track as they slid down his face. Hugging his oldest daughter to him, he cherished the feel of her in his arms. *At least Kim is safe.* She had been inside the house alone with the back door unlocked. *What if whoever had taken— Don't play the what-if game.*

Except for the murder almost a year ago, Crystal Springs was a safe Illinois town. People left their doors unlocked. Kidnappings didn't occur here. Not a lot happened here, and that was one of the reasons he had brought his family back to his hometown after he'd pulled his life out of the gutter.

Kim jerked away and shot to her feet. "I've got to do something to help. I want to search like Neil is. Please, Daddy."

His son had accompanied Reverend Colin Fitzpatrick and a couple of men from the church while they searched the area around Faith Community Church and the lakeshore near it. He hadn't let Kim go with them, partly because she was the last person to see Ashley and needed to be interviewed and partly because he wanted to keep her as close to him as possible. He could have lost her today, too.

"No."

"But I need—"

He planted his hands on his jean-clad thighs and shoved himself to his feet. "I said no, Kim. It's too dark and most of the teams are finishing up."

"Tomorrow then?"

"We'll see. I'm moving the command center to the station, and I want you to come with me." Again he heard thunder in the distance and realized another storm system was moving into the area.

She opened her mouth to say something, decided not to and snapped it closed. After snatching up her jacket on the back of her desk chair, she stalked out into the hallway.

With a heavy sigh, J.T. followed his daughter toward the foyer. The doorbell rang. Kim rushed forward to answer it before he could stop her.

Standing in the entrance to his house was Madison Spencer. The sight of her in her FBI jacket thrust him back to the previous May when murder had come to Crystal Springs. The implication of her presence in town underscored the gravity of the situation and nearly destroyed all the control he had mustered.

TWO

"Madison," J.T. whispered in his entry hall, his voice a weak thread. Seeing the FBI agent jacket cemented in his mind that his daughter wasn't likely to waltz into his house, wanting to eat dinner, anytime soon.

Madison stepped through the doorway. "I'm sorry we're meeting again under lousy circumstances."

Kim looked from Madison to him then back to the agent, her gaze glued to the yellow letters on the navy-blue jacket. "Dad?"

J.T. shook his head at Madison, hoping his brief expression transmitted the need to be careful with what was said. "Honey, the FBI is routinely called in when a child's missing."

But as usual his daughter was smart and observant. "Ashley isn't just missing. Someone took her." Kim's voice and lower lip quivered.

Although it wasn't a question, J.T. answered, "We

don't know for sure—" he stalled, wishing more than anything he didn't have to say the next part of the sentence "—but yes, I think she has been kidnapped."

His daughter bit down on her lip to keep it from trembling. Tears glistened again in her eyes. "Why? Who? We don't have much money."

No words came to mind as he stared at the pain in Kim's expression. Her observation about their financial situation made the fear he'd kept suppressed in order to function effectively bubble to the surface. Financial gain could be handled. The other reasons a child was kidnapped were so much harder as a cop and a parent to deal with. He shuddered. He realized his daughter needed some kind of answer, but he didn't know anything to say that would make the situation better for Kim.

Thankfully Madison stepped forward. "That's what we're going to determine." She steered his daughter toward the couch in the living room. "I can't believe how much you've grown since last summer."

Alone in the foyer, J.T. dropped his head and stared at the ceramic tile. Visions of those other reasons swam around in his numb mind: someone who thrived on sexual exploitation, a person from his past while he was a detective in Chicago, or human traffickers. Another shudder passed through him.

Lord, please bring Ashley home. Protect her. I'm begging You. Help me! I can't lose her. Where do I begin?

The sound of Kim and Madison talking in lowered voices drew him forward. If he was going to do a thorough job of finding his daughter, he had to shut down the thoughts that kept popping into his head. He couldn't waste any more time on them.

"But there hasn't been a ransom demand," Kim said as J.T. entered the room. "There hasn't, has there, Daddy?"

His daughter's big blue gaze fixed upon him chipped away at the composure he had just shored up. "No. Nothing." He instilled strength into his voice, a strength he had to maintain.

"Then, see, she's probably just missing."

"That's a possibility, Kim, but we're covering all the bases until we know something for sure." Madison looked toward the kitchen. "I smell coffee, and I've been driving for a couple of hours. I could use a cup. Do you think you could get me one, Kim?"

"I guess so." His daughter pushed to her feet and trudged across the room, her shoulders hunched.

When she was gone, J.T. came closer to Madison and sat in the chair next to the couch. For some reason her presence helped him feel as though he wasn't totally alone in this. They had worked well last year on the murder case and she was very good at her job. That thought comforted him. "So you left the state police to join the FBI. Where's the rest of the team?"

"They're coming. Probably twenty minutes behind me. I think I broke a few speed limits getting here." She tossed a wry half grin then sobered. "I know what you must—"

"Who's the agent in charge?" He couldn't take her pity and sympathy at the moment. He wasn't *that* strong.

"Matthew Hendricks. He's good at finding people. That's why the Chicago office is handling this instead of the small one in Central City."

Susan came into the living room with a mug. "I talked Kim into eating the ham sandwich I had for her earlier." She handed the coffee to Madison. "Can I get you anything else?"

"No, thanks." Madison sipped her coffee. "This is just what I needed."

"J.T., we've almost got everything packed up to move down to the station. We should be ready to leave in a few minutes." His secretary started back toward the kitchen. "Glad you're here, Madison."

Madison flipped open her cell phone. "I'll call Matthew and let him know to meet us at the sheriff's office on Lake Shore Drive."

While J.T. listened to her talk to the agent in charge, a restless energy hummed through him. He shot to his feet and began to pace. When she finished her call, he stopped in front of her, hands stuffed into his pants' pockets. He remembered her efficiency and professionalism and was glad to see a familiar face.

She took several more sips of her coffee, then placed it on the coaster on the table in front of her. "Okay. That should keep me going. Show me where Ashley was last seen."

"Kim saw her on the swing last, probably right before she was—kidnapped." The word stuck in his throat. Thinking about that shook him to his core. He could have lost both daughters today. Kim had been so close— an unlocked door away. He couldn't get that realization out of his mind.

"What time was that?"

"Kim saw her at about five-thirty. I came home at six-thirty." He recited the facts he'd learned earlier from his daughter as though this was just another case. If he let his emotions rule him, he would fall apart. He couldn't afford that. Not when Ashley's life depended on him keeping a level head.

"So she disappeared some time between five-thirty and six-thirty. We can start building a time frame."

J.T. headed for the front door. "Let's go around to the back this way. If Susan has finally managed to get Kim to eat something, I don't want us to interfere by going through the kitchen."

Madison stepped out onto the small porch first. "Any evidence at the scene?"

"We found one of Ashley's shoes in the grass under a swing." When he followed her, he saw a news crew from Central City setting up in the street behind the barricade his deputies had erected to keep people away from the scene. He had been to hundreds of crime scenes in his career as a law enforcement officer, but never at his own home.

"A tennis shoe? They don't come off easily." Madison strode toward the wooden gate at the side of the house and pushed aside the yellow tape slashed across it.

"No, a slip-on, so in a struggle it could have come off."

"But Kim didn't hear anything?"

"No. She said she checked on Ashley when she first went outside to play, then she moved back to the couch across the room to talk on the phone."

Madison stared into space, a good minute of silence passing. "Still, if there had been much of a struggle, she should have heard something."

"I particularly asked Kim about that. There wasn't anything unusual. All she heard was a dog barking two houses down."

"Which way."

J.T. pointed east. "That way. The Morgans. They have an American Eskimo."

"Maybe the abductor came that way and stirred up the dog. I'll check on that when I interview them."

"I already did. Or rather, I discovered neither Jill nor Ross Morgan were home at that time. Some of the people on the street work in Central City and hadn't gotten home yet."

"Convenient time to take someone."

He massaged the taut muscles in his neck. "Yes, my thinking exactly."

"Do you mind if I interview Kim later? Maybe she'll remember something she's forgotten in the trauma of finding out her sister is missing."

"Sure. I know the drill. We'll do anything to bring Ashley back."

"Has the scene been processed?" She hung back, not going more than a few feet inside the gate.

J.T. came up behind her. "Yes, the crime scene unit from Central City finished about an hour ago."

"That was fast."

"I know the police chief, and I wanted them to start when they at least had some daylight. There wasn't much we found except the shoe and a set of footprints behind there." He indicated the group of trees and bushes along the chain-link fence at the back of the yard. "Most of the area is grassy except for a small spot."

"What size?"

"Cowboy boots, size ten. It rained enough earlier today that it would have washed away any previous prints."

"Did you take a casting?"

He nodded, then realized she couldn't see his answer because she was facing away from him, surveying the yard. "Yes. Ashley had a fort in the bushes. She played there a lot. In fact, when I first came out that was where I thought she was hiding." He gestured toward the largest one that served as Ashley's fort, then toward a chain-link gate not five feet away from it. "There are two ways into the yard."

"So if someone took Ashley, he probably used the back one."

"That's what I'd do. Less chance of being seen since the woods are directly behind my property." A few raindrops spattered him. "Great, more rain."

"Which doesn't help." Madison held her hand out flat as if gauging the intensity of the rain.

J.T. took a step toward the gate. "We fingerprinted the swing set and anything else we could."

"Both gate handles?"

"Yes," he answered in a tight voice as she walked past him. "I know my job. My deputies know their job."

She turned then and stared up at him. "I know, but I still need to ask. You don't want any mistakes in this case. Especially this one. You know how important the crime scene can be." She again scanned the yard. "Even with the lights on, it'll be hard to see anything tonight, especially if it starts raining harder. I'll come back tomorrow. Did your next-door neighbors see anything?"

Madison headed back around front, her short brown hair beginning to get wet.

J.T. hurried his steps. "Nothing. One wasn't even home at the time and the other one is an older lady with a hearing problem. She was watching TV on the far side of the house from four until I knocked on her door at a little before seven."

"So you interviewed all the neighbors on your street?"

J.T. opened his front door and let Madison go into his house first. "There was only one neighbor I didn't talk to. I figured if anyone saw something it would be a neighbor, but no one did."

"Not even an unusual car?"

He shook his head. "Not that anyone can recall. I'll get you copies of the interviews."

"Which neighbor did you not talk to?"

The muscles in his neck ached, pain radiating from his shoulder blades down his back. He again kneaded his nape, but nothing relieved the tightness. "Mrs. Goldsmith left for Central City a little before six to do some shopping and won't be back until probably ten, according to her husband."

"Mr. Goldsmith can't reach her on her cell?"

"She doesn't have a cell."

"Oh." Madison walked through the living room toward the kitchen. "We'll need to talk to her as soon as she returns. She might have seen something and not realized its importance."

"Yeah, I told Bob that. He'll call when she comes home, which should be anytime now."

While Madison went into the kitchen, J.T. hung ba

watching her introduce herself again to Kirk and Rachel, even though they had all worked on last year's murder case together. His daughter sat at the table, a couple of bites taken out of the ham sandwich sitting on a plate before her. Her pale features, too-shiny eyes and hunched shoulders revealed the strain the past few hours had taken on her. Unless Ashley was found soon, he knew the stress had only just begun.

"Besides canvasing the neighborhood, what other searches have been done?"

Although Madison had asked Kirk the question, J.T. moved into the room and said, "We have searched the usual places kids like to hang out and any place Ashley is familiar with. We have checked with all her friends and classmates."

Madison turned toward him as a flash of lightning, followed almost immediately by a clap of thunder, rocked the house. "How about the area behind your yard?"

With a box in his hands, Kirk skirted around Madison and headed toward the front of the house. "I'm in charge of organizing a search of that area all the way to the lake and the lake itself first thing tomorrow morning. The terrain is rough and would be difficult to search properly in the dark even with lights. We've got some firefighters and police coming from Central City to help us. We'll be using Central City's K-9 unit along with some search-and-rescue teams. They should be here an hour or so before dawn. Hopefully the rain will let up by then. That's what the weather report says."

"Isn't it likely if there was a kidnapper, that he took her

out that way since none of the neighbors saw anything unusual?" Madison asked Kirk as she trailed after him.

In the living room away from Kim, J.T. caught Madison's arm and halted her progress. Another rumble of thunder vibrated the air. Tension whipped down his length. "There's no *if* in this. Ashley has been kidnapped."

Madison glanced down at his hand on her then back up into his eyes. He instantly dropped his arm away as though touching her had burned him.

"I agree this is most likely a kidnapping, J.T. Until we discover otherwise, our standard procedure is to assume a child is in immediate danger and act accordingly. It's better to do that rather than think she's missing or a runaway. We don't want to miss any clues."

She was giving him information he already knew, but he realized it was her way of keeping a rein on his emotions, which could so easily run rampant if he allowed them. "I want to make sure we're on the same page."

She stepped closer and laid her hand on his arm, the touch meant to reassure. Strangely it did. "We are. I promise you we'll do everything humanly possible to bring your daughter home."

Day one, 5:00 a.m.: Ashley missing for ten and a half hours

Madison scrubbed her hands down her face. Her eyes stung from the sleepless night spent at the sheriff's office, now the command center for the missing child case. The rest of the FBI agents had arrived right after they had moved to the station to set up the new command post away from the victim's house.

Just the mere thought of the word *victim,* in reference to J.T.'s little girl, chilled Madison. She couldn't even begin to imagine the anguish J.T. and his family were going through, and yet he was in the middle of the investigation as though the child missing was someone else's. Professional. Staunch.

She'd tried to get him to back off and let his deputies and the FBI work the case, but he wouldn't. Since he was the sheriff as well as the parent, he wanted to be in on it every step of the way. There was a part of her that understood his need, and yet she also knew the danger of being so emotionally invested in a case. Ashley wasn't her child, but she knew the little girl from the summer before. J.T. and his family had made her feel welcome when she had been here with this department working on the murder. Her emotions were involved more than she wished.

Madison found J.T. standing in front of the time line her boss had constructed on a large dry erase board. At the moment there was little information about Ashley posted. The bleak look in J.T.'s expression spoke of how taxing the situation was for him. But he was going over the information on the board with Matthew Hendricks as though this wasn't his daughter they were discussing.

J.T.'s faith was strong like hers. Was that what was holding him together? What a test of his faith! Throughout the past night she'd prayed silently on a number of occasions for Ashley's safe return. From the distant look that would appear from time to time in J.T.'s eyes, she suspected he had, too.

Heavenly Father, give us some kind of direction. We've got everything set up and ready to go but no leads to speak of. Where do we start? Where do we go from here?

"I made some fresh coffee." Susan placed a steaming mug in front of Madison. "That's the least I can do since I returned to the station. There's no arguing with J.T. when he sets his mind on something. I didn't want to go home to sleep."

"A few people needed to get some sleep. I hope you were able to." Madison put her hands around the warm mug.

"Not much, but I did manage to close my eyes for a while. Then I'd see Ashley's face and I just couldn't get any sleep. She is so dear and sweet. J.T. dotes on her. You should see them together when she comes down to the station. Such patience, showing her what he does. I just don't understand how someone could take—" Distress on her face, Susan shook her head. "Sorry. I shouldn't go on like that. And certainly J.T. doesn't need to hear me carrying on. He's got enough to deal with."

"I don't see how anyone could ever take a child, but it happens and the parents' lives are never the same."

"Even when the child is found?"

"Their sense of security is stripped away."

A thoughtful expression appeared on Susan's face. "Ah, I never considered that."

The aroma of the brew flavored the air and for a few seconds Madison shut her eyes and relished the smell. "Thanks for the coffee. I was about to tape my eyelids open."

J.T.'s secretary chuckled. "I know the feeling. It's been a long night for everyone here."

"And today will be a long day." Madison rose from the desk she had commandeered from one of the deputies. "How's J.T. holding up?" She'd been reviewing the neighbors' statements and had been working on a list of people to interview again while J.T., her boss and Kirk had finalized the search protocol and gone over the case to date.

"I don't know how he keeps going. I would have fallen apart hours ago." Susan walked to the next desk to hand one of the FBI agents a mug of coffee.

Madison again searched for J.T. in the large room, realizing that periodically throughout the night she had done that very thing. By the time she'd left last summer they had become friends. She hated seeing a friend going through such pain. She wished she could do more for him.

J.T. moved away from the dry erase board and stopped in front of a table where a map of the region was spread out. He pointed to an area and said something to Matthew. The lead agent nodded, then gestured to another place.

Exhaustion carved deep lines into J.T.'s face—a face that under normal circumstances had a lot of character. At the moment it just looked plain tired. Even in the middle of the murder investigation last year, J.T.'s gray eyes would sparkle with life and humor. What she saw now was a dull pewter color. A sudden urge to comfort him flooded her. Surprised by the emotion, she turned away and picked up her list to give to Rachel.

"These are the people I want to interview again, with Mrs. Goldsmith at the top."

Rachel glanced up. "She usually gets up early."

"So six-thirty won't be too early then?"

"Nope, and knowing Mrs. Goldsmith, she wouldn't mind being awakened—if she even got any rest."

"I suspect there are a lot of townspeople who aren't sleeping right now."

"Yeah, J.T. is a good sheriff and friend to many." Rachel clicked the computer program she was working in shut. "You aren't going to participate in the search of the lake area?"

"Not until I've interviewed all these people. They may remember something they didn't last night."

"Do you want me to come with you?"

"No, I'm sure even with the added volunteers from Central City J.T. could use everyone possible to help in the search. He'll need you there."

"First, I've got to finish up here. Then I plan on being in the thick of things. I'd do anything for J.T. He believed in me when no one else did."

"He did?"

"Yeah, I'd always wanted to be a law enforcement officer, but no one around here thought I would be any good. Too petite, not to mention the fact I'm a woman."

"I always wanted to be in law enforcement, too."

"It wasn't easy at first. I had to prove myself, but each one of these guys is my friend now. Everyone at the station would do anything for J.T. and his little girl."

She knew what Rachel meant. She could feel the respect and friendship when she watched J.T. work with his staff. She hadn't been with the FBI long enough to form that kind of bond yet. She was the one who was the new kid on the block and had to prove herself.

Madison peered over her shoulder at J.T. He now stood at the window with the blinds open. With his coffee mug cupped between his hands, he stared into the dark, as though holding vigil until dawn appeared. His lonely vulnerability drew her across the room. They had less than an hour until the sun came up and everything that could be done had been done. Now they just had to wait for dawn.

His rigid stance told Madison more than words what a toll the past hours had taken on J.T. Susan might think he was holding himself together, but Madison knew it was a very fragile connection that any second could give way.

She came up beside him with her own mug nestled in her hands, relishing the heat that warmed her cold body. She faced the darkness and saw their reflections. He was only a few inches taller than her five feet eleven inches, but where she was slender, almost reed thin, he was broad shouldered and muscular.

Madison remembered J.T.'s two older children reluctantly agreeing to go home with Reverend Colin Fitzpatrick and his wife, Emma, to get some rest. She'd also seen the silent struggle waging within J.T. Did he allow his children to go or stay with him where he could keep an eye on them, possibly protect them from whomever had taken Ashley? J.T. was sure his youngest daughter had been kidnapped, and after going over what evidence they had, she agreed. Deep down it felt like an abduction.

She turned toward him, her arm brushing against his. The brief contact riveted her attention on him, causing a catch in her throat. "I'm glad the rain finally stopped a while ago."

"Yeah." J.T. sipped his coffee.

"Did you have a chance to talk with Colin when he picked up Kim and Neil?"

"Just a few minutes. He's bringing my son back at dawn, so Neil can help with the search."

"How about Kim? I want to talk to her again."

"Emma will stay with her at Grace's house. Between those two they should be able to—" he cleared his throat "—take care of her, keep her safe."

"If I recall correctly, Grace was a drill sergeant in the army before she retired."

"Yes. I have to know Kim's in good hands or—" He worked his mouth but no other words would come out.

A tightness clogged her own throat. She put her mug on the windowsill and faced him. "Let us take care of everything. I don't know how you're keeping yourself together." She reached out and touched his arm, wishing she could take his pain away, wishing she could do so much more.

His muscles tightened beneath her fingertips. His gaze bore into her. "No! My daughter is missing. I will bring her home." His mouth firmed into a fierce expression. "You don't need to worry about me falling apart. I won't allow it. I have the most important job of my life to do and nothing will stand in my way." His savage tone, directed more at the situation than at her, never rose above a loud whisper.

When he brought his mug to his lips, her fingers slipped from his arm, but not before she noticed the hand holding his coffee quivered slightly. "We all have a breaking point."

Over the rim of his cup, he glared at her but didn't say a word.

Determined to make him see he had his limits, she didn't back down from him. "I'm available if you need someone to talk to. And I'm sure Colin is, too."

"I know." The hardness in his features melted some. "I know you're worried, but don't be. I haven't been a sheriff of a small town all my career. I've seen bad situations before."

"But none that involved your own family."

A distant look flared in his eyes as though a memory surfaced, best left in the past. "I know what I have to do, Madison. I won't fail Ashley."

His professional facade, locked in place, shut down any further discussion about how this was affecting him. Madison drew in a calming breath. "Okay. Then let's talk business for a moment. I see Eric Carlton on the list of people you interviewed, but nothing was written down under his name. Why?"

"Because we couldn't find him. I have two deputies out looking for him right now. He's the only person in Crystal Springs that has been convicted of a sex crime. He lives outside of town near the lake. One of the teams with a dog from the K-9 unit will be concentrating around his cabin."

"Then he's your prime suspect at the moment?" Although she felt out of the loop, she had to remember she was just one agent and could do only so much. For the past hours she had concentrated on going over what physical evidence they had, then looking at all the logs of the interviews so she could talk with each person and possibly discover something that could help the investigation.

"The only suspect at the moment unless you count all the people I've put away who are now out of prison. Your boss has one of your agents over at Carlton's cabin waiting for him in case he decides to return home."

"Do you think he will? Or will he flee?"

"I think he's long gone. I put an APB out on him and his black Ford truck. Maybe we'll get lucky and someone will pick him up."

"How about any other sex offenders from the surrounding towns or Central City?" He flinched as she asked the question which had to be asked. The thought of a sex offender having Ashley terrified her, so she could imagine how J.T. felt.

"I have Rachel working on that."

She studied his thoughtful expression, his creased forehead. "But you don't think that's it?"

He looked long and hard at her. "No. Someone came into my yard and took Ashley, probably through my back gate that leads to the woods and lake. It feels calculated to me."

"So you'll start the search at your back gate?"

"No, the swing set, although I think the trail will lead to the back gate. Our goal will be twofold. We'll look for any evidence left behind and for a trail that leads to Ashley's whereabouts." His gaze shifted to the window. "Last night before it become totally dark, I checked out the immediate area by my gate. I didn't see anything, but the shadows could have hidden something."

Madison twisted around and saw the shift in the degree of darkness. "While you're searching, I'm going to canvass your neighbors again, especially Mrs. Goldsmith. Maybe she'll remember something about that car she saw pull out of the side street near your house. After that I want to talk with Kim."

He squeezed his eyes closed for a few seconds. "She's not taking this well. She blames herself. I'm hoping Colin can help her. He's especially good with teens."

"Are you blaming yourself?"

He stiffened. "Kinda hard not to. I think someone from my past has decided to make me pay for putting him behind bars. While working in Chicago, I received some threats, usually when the criminals had been convicted and were going to prison. They like to blame the cop who caught them rather than themselves."

Her heart broke at the desolate expression on his face. "Is anyone making a list of people you caught who are now out of prison?" In Chicago when she'd jumped at the chance to return to Crystal Springs to help find J.T.'s daughter, she hadn't realized how hard it was going to be to keep herself from becoming emotionally involved. Nearly impossible.

"Rachel. She's good with the computer."

"I want both her lists when they are compiled."

After he put his mug next to hers on the sill, he rolled his shoulders then worked the kinks out of his neck. "Let her know. If the search doesn't produce anything, that's where I'll be concentrating next."

"You know, something is bothering me about this whole situation."

He slid his gaze to her, his head tilted. "What?"

"From the gate at the back of your yard to the swing set is a good twenty feet. If a stranger had come into the yard, wouldn't Ashley have reacted? Screamed or something? Which means Kim or a neighbor would have heard her."

His eyes widened. "You've got a point." He glanced behind him at the throng of people in the large room, all waiting for the first rays of light. "That would mean the person who took her was someone she knew and possibly trusted." The hand he pushed through his hair trembled.

"It's something we need to consider."

"Which would blow my theory out of the water. Because I know no one in this town has been in prison because of me. I grew up in Crystal Springs. I came back here five years ago and I know everyone. I have a hard time believing it could be someone I know. It's more likely an ex-con."

"The evidence says otherwise. Prove me wrong."

He straightened. "I will."

The door to the sheriff's office opened and Colin, followed by Neil, came into the station. J.T.'s eighteen-year-old son looked almost as bad as his father. Dark circles under his eyes gave him a haunted look. And from Colin's appearance, Madison surmised no one got any rest at the Fitzpatrick household.

J.T. strode toward the pair and enveloped his son in a bear hug, patting him on the back. Madison stayed off to the side for a few seconds while father and son exchanged some words. When she finally approached the threesome, both J.T. and Neil had their emotions under control.

"Dad, any news?"

J.T. shook his head.

"No ransom demand?"

"No, son."

Neil perked up. "Then Ashley might just be missing."

"That's a possibility."

The way J.T. had said the sentence left no doubt in Madison's mind that it was a distant possibility, and his son picked up on that fact. Last year during the murder investigation J.T. would never have allowed his tone of voice to give any hint of what he was thinking unless he had wanted it that way. Now however, exhaustion and a father's love had stripped him of his usual defenses.

"You don't think it is, do you, Dad?"

"I'm not gonna lie to you. No, I don't."

"But if the person doesn't want money, what…" All the color drained from Neil's face. He collapsed back against the desk behind him and clutched its edge to keep himself upright. Tears sprang to his eyes.

J.T. grasped his son's shoulders and forced Neil to look him in the eye. "Nothing is going to happen to Ashley. I will bring her home alive and safe. I won't lie to you and I won't mince words with you. I think some felon from my past has taken Ashley to get back at me."

"Then she could be dead," Neil said in a raw whisper.

"No!" J.T. pulled away and placed his fist over his heart. "I would know in here. She's alive."

As J.T. talked with Neil in a low voice, their heads bowed in prayer, Madison moved to Colin's side. The emotional impact from the brief encounter between father and son left her reeling.

"Okay?"

The reverend's question forced her to acknowledge what this case was doing to her. "No, I'm having a hard time distancing myself from this one. I wanted to come to Crystal Springs to help in the search for Ashley, but maybe I shouldn't have." The constriction in her chest rose into her throat. "His pain—it must be unbearable." She twisted toward Colin. "If I'm having this much trouble keeping my personal feelings under control, how in the world is J.T. going to manage to keep his professional perspective?"

"One moment at a time. That's all he can do. He knows God is with him and will take the burden from his shoulders. They will face it as one." Colin took her hands. "The Lord has already eased J.T.'s load. He brought you here to help. You two worked well together last year."

Madison glanced over at J.T. and saw him put an arm around his son's shoulder. She prayed the reverend was right. A little girl's life hung in the balance.

THREE

Day one, 6:00 a.m.: Ashley missing eleven and a half hours

Wisps of fog fingered their way through the trees, reaching toward the lake like claws digging at the earth. J.T. stood at his back gate, his skin clammy from the cool, damp spring air. The searchers had received their instructions and Ashley's denim jacket for the dogs to get her scent. The teams had begun to move forward from his property line through the woods because the trail from the swing set led to the back gate. That only confirmed in J.T.'s mind he was on the right track.

A handler from Central City, a young police officer J.T. had worked with before, held Ashley's jacket up to his German shepherd. After a few sniffs, his dog took off to the right into the forest.

J.T. hurried after the dog and his handler. The German shepherd stopped at the base of an elm and smelled its trunk. In the distance J.T. heard another dog bark.

Although he knew this wasn't a viable lead, J.T.

checked the area around the tree just to be sure. "Dead end. Ashley often comes out here and climbs this tree. She's been wanting me to build her a fort in—".The rest of the words couldn't get past the knot lodged in J.T.'s throat. He might never get the opportunity to build that fort he'd kept putting off. If only he had another chance…

Day one, 6:30 a.m.: Ashley missing twelve hours

Madison rang the Goldsmiths' doorbell, scanned J.T.'s neighborhood. A white Escort sat in the neighbors' driveway. People headed toward the side street where the volunteers were signing in. The barricade in front of J.T.'s house still stood, proclaiming a crime had been committed. Several reporters milled about, looking for people to interview. Thankfully she'd been able to evade them.

Behind her she heard the door open and turned toward an older man. She showed him her FBI badge. "I would like to talk to Mrs. Goldsmith."

"I was just about to call the sheriff."

"Why?"

"Ruth remembered some more about that car she saw pulling out of the side street yesterday evening." He stood to the side to allow her into his house.

A muscular woman, medium height, came into the foyer from what looked like the living room. She stuck out her hand.

Madison shook it, noticing the scent of vanilla permeating the house. "What did you remember about the car?"

"I've been baking sugar cookies. I do that when I need to think." Ruth turned back into the room. "Come in and have some coffee."

Madison glanced at her watch. Minutes ticked by faster than she wanted. The longer Ashley was missing, the harder it would be to find her—alive. That thought prompted her to say, "I can't, but thanks for the offer. I have a lot of people to interview this morning." She took several steps into the room. "What do you remember, Mrs. Goldsmith?"

"Ruth. The color was definitely a metallic blue, not gray as I thought last night."

Madison nodded, remembering that from the report she'd read. She bit down on the inside of her cheek as Ruth sat again on the couch and brought her mug to her lips.

"The thing is I'm almost positive the first three numbers of the license were five, one, three."

"How positive?" Madison wrote the numbers down on her pad, trying not to get too excited.

Ruth leaned forward and set her mug on a magazine. Then she sat back straight and looked right at Madison. "Positive. I was thinking those numbers were today's date. Well, yesterday I was thinking tomorrow's date."

"Do you recall the make of the car?"

"Big. I'm not good with the different kinds of cars."

"Yep, Ruth thinks a car is either big or small." Mr. Goldsmith took the seat next to her on the couch and patted her knee.

"Anything else? Did you recognize who was driving?"

"Nope. The windows were tinted dark. Couldn't see too well inside and besides, whoever was driving sped away."

"Speeding? You didn't say anything about that last night."

"All I could think about last night was that Ashley was missing. That poor child. I've got to fix something for J.T.'s family to eat. They will need to eat during this ordeal."

"Yes, ma'am. They will." Madison finished putting the information down on her pad. "Is that all? You might close your eyes…" When the woman did, Madison continued, "…and try to picture the car driving away."

Ruth popped one eye open. "You mean speeding away."

"Yes."

The fiftysomething woman closed both eyes again. An almost tranquil expression descended on her lined face. Suddenly she looked right at Madison. "Nope. Nothing, but if I remember anything else, I'll give you a call."

Madison removed one of her cards and jotted down her cell number. "You can reach me here day or night."

The second Madison stepped out onto the Goldsmiths' front porch and the door closed behind her, she punched in the sheriff's number. When the deputy on duty at the office answered, she gave him the description of the car with the partial Illinois license plate number. "It's important we find the driver. The car was seen speeding away from the area about the time of the abduction."

Day one, 6:30 a.m.: Ashley missing twelve hours

As J.T. made his way through the woods toward the back gate with the K-9 police officer and his German shepherd, a dog's bark echoed through the trees repeatedly.

"We found something," a searcher shouted.

J.T. glanced in the direction and hurried his steps as a crime scene tech reached the dog who sat next to his handler. After the tech took a photograph, J.T. saw him pick up Ashley's pink socks with butterflies and put them into a plastic bag. His heart slowed to a painful throb. Then the young man removed a wet, pale pink T-shirt from the ground behind a bush.

For a few seconds everything came to a standstill for J.T. The woods swam before his eyes and he staggered a couple of steps.

Focus!

He drew in a breath that didn't fill his lungs. Again he inhaled the moisture-rich air until finally he didn't feel so light-headed. Careful where he walked, J.T. made his way toward the crime-scene tech who now was bagging his daughter's blue jeans with butterflies around the hem. Sweat popped out on J.T.'s forehead and seemed instantly to drench him as he spied Ashley's outer clothing in separate evidence bags lined up on the ground. That sight nearly brought him to his knees.

Was Ashley sexually assaulted?

The young man held up a smaller plastic container. "It looks like he used a tranquilizer dart to neutralize her."

J.T. clenched his jaw to keep the words, "That's my daughter you're talking about," from spilling out. He steadied himself and took the bag with the dart and examined it.

Is this why Kim didn't hear anything? Why Ashley didn't scream?

Day one, 7:00 a.m.: Ashley missing twelve and a half hours

"Colin told me you were working on the case." Emma Fitzpatrick let Madison into her house.

"I wouldn't have had it any other way when I heard about Ashley missing." Madison scanned the familiar foyer, remembering back to the time she had worked with J.T. on Emma's brother's murder case.

"You're here to see Kim?"

"Yes. I want to talk to her. Is she up?"

"Actually, I doubt she slept any last night even though she went to bed. She's in the kitchen with Grace. We were fixing breakfast. We're trying to get her to eat something." Emma started for the back of the house. "Have you eaten yet?"

"No, but—"

"If I discovered anything from my trauma last year, it was that a person has to take care of herself if she's going to do her best job."

"You're beginning to sound like Grace."

Emma slanted a glance over her shoulder. "I'll take that as a compliment."

"You should." When Madison entered the kitchen, Grace greeted her with a smile and a mug of coffee. "I heard you coming and remembered you like your cup of joe black."

A night of no sleep was beginning to catch up with her. Madison drank some of the brew, wondering when she would turn into a huge cup of coffee. "Thanks. This tastes wonderful, Grace." Then turning to the teenager at the table, her gaze riveted to the window overlooking the backyard, Madison added, "I came to see you, Kim. I'd like to ask you a few questions."

"I told Dad and Rachel what happened."

The waver in the girl's voice italicized the fragile control she had over her emotions. Madison noted that as she sat across from her and placed her mug on the table. "I know. But sometimes when you retell an event, it triggers a memory you forgot."

"Nope. I told them everything." Kim shifted her attention to Madison, a dullness in her gaze. "I told Ashley to go outside and play while I talked with Lexie. It had stopped raining and the sun had even peeked out of the clouds. I checked on her as she went to the swing and sat down, then I took a seat on the couch again and talked until I heard Dad come home." Hopelessness rang in the rote recitation of the facts.

"You didn't see anything out of place in the backyard?" Madison asked, concerned by both Kim's apathetic tone and her appearance, as though she had wakened from a nap and hadn't bothered to comb her hair.

The teenager shook her head. Suddenly her lower lip quivered while tears flooded her eyes and a look of devastation took hold of Kim.

"It isn't your fault," Madison said, knowing from

J.T. that Kim blamed herself for Ashley's disappearance. Blame was such a wasted emotion, but she almost always saw it in this type of situation. The "if onlys" could eat at a person until there was nothing left.

Kim blinked, loosening a tear to slide down her cheek. "You don't understand. I screamed at Ashley to leave me alone. Daddy doesn't think so, but I think she ran away because of me. What if she fell and hurt herself so that's why she hasn't come home?"

Madison wished that was the case, but more and more she felt J.T. was right. Ashley had been abducted. "As we speak there are search dogs and teams of people out looking for Ashley. If that happened, they'll find her."

Suddenly Kim reached across the table and clutched Madison's hand. "I need to help in the search. Make Daddy see that. Please."

The desperation in the girl's voice tore at Madison's composure. Knowing the people involved in this tragedy made her job doubly hard but doubly important, too. "Kim, I want you to think back to yesterday. Close your eyes if it will help you visualize the scene with Ashley in the backyard." After the teenager did as she was instructed, Madison continued, "Now, do you see anything unusual, anything out of place?"

A long minute passed with a heavy silence filling the air, spiced with the aromas of bacon and biscuits.

When Kim opened her eyes, her forehead wrinkled and she tilted her head to the side, as J.T. did when he was thinking. "There was something shiny by the bushes along the back of the fence where Ashley's fort is."

"Could you tell what it is?"

"No," the girl answered slowly, then more definitely, "No."

The ringing of Madison's cell phone pierced the quiet. She quickly answered it.

"It's J.T. I told you I would call if we found anything. We discovered Ashley's clothing in a pile behind a set of bushes forty feet from the back gate. There was a dart from a tranquilizer gun at the bottom of the pile. That's why Kim didn't hear a scream from Ashley. We're bringing in a cadaver search dog."

The implication of bringing in a dog that specialized in finding dead bodies, even ones buried in the ground, caused her to draw in a sharp breath. "I'll be right there."

Day one, 7:30 a.m.: Ashley missing thirteen hours

Madison hurried to the area where some of Ashley's clothing had been found. She stopped at the perimeter of the taped-off section, spying J.T. directly across from her about fifteen yards away. The grim look on his face as he watched the crime scene techs process the evidence and comb the ground for any more clues highlighted the anguish he had to be feeling, standing to the side, unable to do anything but watch.

She skirted the edge of the taped area and came to his side. "Have they found anything else?"

"No," he said in such a tight voice she was afraid he would shatter any second. "Finding her clothes, folded in a neat pile, like that—" His voice came to an abrupt halt, his jaw clenched so tight a nerve twitched on his face.

Why would the kidnapper remove Ashley's clothes,

leave them here for them to find? Was it some kind of ritual he needed to perform? Was he toying with J.T., trying to break him? Was the little girl molested? Question after question bombarded Madison, with no real answers. The only thing she knew was the effect it was having on J.T. Color leached from his normally tanned features and the despair in his expression as he watched one of the crime scene techs remove the evidence bags to their van illuminated how effective the kidnapper's technique was if he was after revenge.

She didn't care that they were standing among a swarm of people. She took hold of his hand, hoping to impart some support. He needed to know he wasn't alone through this. "We may be able to find some clues on the clothes that will help us."

He closed his eyes for a long moment as though he had to shut out the scene around him in order to keep going. "The kidnapper came prepared. He brought a tranquilizer dart to silence Ashley. As I suspected, this wasn't spur-of-the-moment. He planned it, possibly for years while he was in jail."

J.T. was so positive it was a criminal he had put in jail, and frankly she was beginning to think that was the most likely prospect. This case was becoming more personal as the hours passed.

He turned toward her, breaking their linked hands apart. "Another search team found a trail off to the left that ended at the road. But I don't know if that means Ashley was taken in a car somewhere or if she went that way to play sometime recently." Frustration marked his face.

"The trouble is her scent is all over the place. She loved to play here which isn't making it easy for the dogs."

"When will the cadaver search dog be here?"

He checked his watch. "A half hour. I should have had it here from the beginning. It's just…" Not finishing his statement, he snapped his jaw closed, every line of his body conveying the anxiety that gripped him.

Madison lay her hand on his arm, hoping to draw his attention to her and away from the techs still working the crime scene. Again she wished she could take some of his pain away and felt helpless because she couldn't. No one could but God. J.T. faced the bushes where Ashley's clothes were found, his mouth set in a frown.

"It's rough having to admit the possibility there could be a body. You weren't thinking along those lines." She gently squeezed his arm, imparting her support the best way she could.

"I need to think more and feel less."

She moved in front of him and blocked his view, forcing him to look at her. The brief anger that flashed into his eyes dissolved into a solemn expression. "No matter how much you want to be totally the sheriff right now you won't be able to do that. It's not possible to forget you're the parent as much as you would like to. We all understand."

The tic in his jawline increased its twitching. "How do you know what I'm going through?" He swept his arm wide to indicate the people around them. "How do any of them know?"

"This isn't my first missing child case, J.T. Matthew Hendricks has dealt with quite a few abductions in his career. We're here to help, and as much as we can, we do understand what you're going through."

"Then understand this. It's the sheriff in me that will bring my daughter home safely." He pointed toward where the clothes had been found. "All I want to do right now is begin digging with my bare hands everywhere nearby until I find her—" he swallowed hard "—or there's no place left to dig."

As a career law enforcement officer he knew the importance of processing the scene first, but whether he wanted to admit it or not, his emotions were involved in this case and if he wasn't careful that could become a big problem. "They might discover something to help us. When we find this guy we want the evidence to be sound, not tainted," she said as a gentle reminder of what the crime scene techs were doing at that very moment, even though it took precious minutes away from searching the area.

He sent her a look that iced her blood as though he were saying the man responsible would never be taken alive. Again the urge to help in more ways than she was already flooded Madison. Was Colin right? She was beginning to wonder if the Lord had led her to this case because J.T. needed someone to be there for him through the ordeal—someone who could understand the pull he was experiencing. He was a sheriff, and from all she knew a good one, but he was also a parent who desperately wanted to protect his family even to the point of taking the law into his own hands. She couldn't allow him to do that. He would pay for that the rest of his life.

She smiled, pointing toward the direction she had

come in. "C'mon. I noticed Susan at the staging area. She's got some doughnuts and coffee. You need to eat something."

J.T. sidestepped so she didn't block his view. "I need to stay here."

She got in front of him again and thrust her face close to his. "You need to take care of yourself or what good will you be to Ashley?"

His glare snagged hers. "I can't eat at a time like this!"

She didn't back down. She toughened her expression and voice. "You know how important it is for the family, especially the parents, to take care of themselves through an ordeal like this. That goes for you, too. Just because you're the sheriff doesn't make it any less important. What good can you do if you collapse from exhaustion and lack of food?"

His mouth slashed down in a frown. "I'll go, but as soon as the dog arrives, I'm returning."

"And I'll come with you."

He started walking toward the staging area where Susan manned the table, signing in the search volunteers. "I thought Matthew assigned you to interview everyone again."

"He did and I will, but I need to be here in case…" She couldn't quite say, "In case the dog finds Ashley's body." She still had hope that the child was alive and possibly would be found soon.

J.T. cleared his throat. "How are your interviews coming?"

"I've talked with Ruth Goldsmith and Kim. I'll finish the others after we see what happens here."

"Did either one remember anything else?"

"Mrs. Goldsmith thinks she remembers the first three license plate numbers on the car speeding out of the side street about the time the abduction would have occurred. I've got the deputy back at the station working on it."

J.T. halted and stared at her. Hope blazed for a few seconds. "That might be just what we need to break this case wide-open. If she had only remembered that last night."

As much as she and J.T. wished differently, witnesses didn't always recall details right away especially when first confronted with the fact a crime had been committed. "From the report she was pretty upset when she heard about Ashley last night."

He stared forward again. "I know. She was good to Ashley. My daughter liked to visit her."

"Kim remembers seeing a shiny flash from the fort area."

"The sun glinting off something?"

"Maybe."

When they arrived at the area where the volunteers signed in and got their assigned sector, Madison made her way to the table with the coffee and doughnuts on it. She poured J.T. a cup and gave it to him. His fingers brushed against hers as he took it. The contact jolted her. Stunned at her reaction in the midst of everything going on, she jerked her hand back. While she fixed her cup, J.T. grabbed a doughnut, passed it to her, then retrieved one for himself.

"What a cliché." He gestured to his doughnut.

"But how would people know we were officers if we

didn't have them?" She lifted the glazed sweet. "Cop. Doughnut. They go hand in hand."

His chuckle peppered the air for a few seconds before he sobered, his eyes round as though he was shocked that he could find humor when his life was falling apart.

She leaned close. "It's okay to laugh. It's good for the soul, especially in times like this." She quickly pulled back when she smelled his woody scent mingled with the coffee aroma. "Now eat up. We wouldn't want to disappoint all those people who think all cops eat for breakfast are doughnuts."

The sweetness of the glazed delight melted in her mouth and she relished it. She needed the energy boost of carbohydrates because she felt the effects of being up for over twenty-four hours. As she ate her doughnut and drank her coffee, she made sure that J.T. did, too. Dutifully, he finished one and grabbed another.

Susan approached the urn and refilled her cup. "I've checked in all the volunteers. I even had to turn some away. I told them they could help with making posters and putting them up around town. Boss, why did I have to write down everyone's name who's helping and their contact information? I should have been on a team looking for Ashley."

J.T. peered at the area where they had found his daughter's clothing. "Like some arsonists, a kidnapper sometimes likes to return and help out with the search. It's good to have that information in case we need it later."

With her eyes saucer round, Susan said, "You're kidding! Then I'm glad I could help. I want to get this monster."

"We will," J.T. whispered in a roughened voice.

If it's the last thing he does, Madison added silently, seeing that look again in his darkened eyes.

Susan took a sip of her brew. "What else can I do now? Join a search team? Make posters?"

"Go back and help at the station. You're pretty good with the computer. I need the list of criminals I put in jail finished in case nothing pans out here. Rachel has been working on it."

"I should help here. There's a lot of ground to cover."

J.T. plucked the cup out of Susan's hand. "Go. Sit at a computer and let your fingers do the searching."

"But—"

"Susan, you look tired. I bet when I sent you home last night you didn't get any rest. Come back this afternoon. You've been great organizing the volunteers. I may need you later."

She took her cup out of his hand. "Then I could use this if I'm gonna make it to the station."

Madison watched the older woman walk away, her large, thin frame wilting as though she had held herself together until J.T. had given her permission to admit her exhaustion. "She's efficient."

"Since she came to Crystal Springs two years ago, my office actually runs effortlessly. She's more than efficient. I'm not an organized person. Thankfully, Susan is."

"And you worry about her?"

"She's nearly fifty-eight and had some health issues this past year. She even had to take some time off lately. I don't want her to get sick because she didn't take care of herself. I don't need that on my conscience, too."

No, he didn't, but Madison wasn't sure that would stop the guilt from manifesting itself. He was so vulnerable right now. "All your staff is good, J.T. I remember that from last year." She could have added that the reason he had such a good staff was because of him. But J.T. wouldn't like her to say that. Last year she'd discovered compliments didn't sit well with him.

"Well, right now I wish Ted was back from his vacation."

Madison knew that Ted was J.T.'s right-hand man. They worked well together. "Have you thought of calling him and letting him know what's going on?"

"Yes, but I won't. He deserves the time off, and besides, he's sitting on an island in the Caribbean. He saved for this trip for several years. I won't cut it short for him."

"When was the last time you had a vacation?" Madison popped the last bite of her doughnut into her mouth.

"Three years ago. I took the family out to the Badlands. We camped out and saw the sights. Ashley was a little young but…"

"But what?"

He squeezed his eyes close for a few seconds. "She was a trouper as always."

"We'll bring her home." She hoped if she said it enough it would come true.

"But how?" He stared at something beyond her shoulder.

Madison pivoted and saw a man with a dog on a leash making a direct path for them. "That's the cadaver search dog?"

A curt nod of J.T.'s head accentuated the meaning of

bringing in such a dog. Her stomach clenched with the implication. Finding the clothes made it clear this was an abduction. The fact they had been folded in a neat stack, just waiting for someone to find them sent a chill through Madison. Someone wanted J.T. to suffer. Why?

"If my daughter is in the woods, Jasper will find her."

Darkness enveloped her like a heavy blanket thrown over her head. Ashley lay on a smelly cot that reminded her of a pile of dirty clothes in her brother's room. Thinking of Neil brought tears to her eyes. She knuckled them away and swung her legs over the edge of her bed. Her bare feet touched the coldness of the cement floor. She instantly scooted back against the wall that trapped the cold, too. When she brought her pajama-clad legs up, she curled her arms around them and hugged them to her, seeking any warmth she could.

Where are my clothes?

I wanna go home.

Where's Daddy? Why hasn't he come to get me?

Because the bad man had her, locked in a basement where her daddy couldn't find her.

Click.

Ashley tensed, flattening herself against the cold wall. Icy shivers snaked down her spine. An opening slid back. A shaft of light from above flooded her inky surroundings. She blinked at its intrusion.

Her gaze fixed on the doggy-sized door in the bigger one, she waited for her tray of food to be delivered. When it appeared on the top stair, a dim overhead light flicked on. The opening banged shut.

Hunger twisted her stomach. Thirst dried her mouth. She only had a little while to eat before the dark returned. She raced across the small room and flew up the stairs to grab the tray. She stuffed the peanut butter sandwich into her mouth and gulped down the lukewarm water. She didn't want to be on the steps when the light went out like the time before when she was given some food by a stranger.

With her last bite, she wiped the back of her hand across her mouth as she finished chewing. She studied the small opening and wondered if she could fit through it and escape. She started to investigate it then remembered the dark. Not enough time.

She hurried down the steps. As the lights blinked off, her feet connected with the ice-cold cement. Blackness engulfed her.

"No! Don't! I'll be good."

Tears sprang to her eyes and ran down her cheeks. She wanted to curl into a ball on the floor and pray this was all a bad dream. But the cold from the floor made her teeth chatter. This wasn't a nightmare. This was real.

With arms stretched out, she slowly crossed the remaining distance to her cot. Her safe haven. She sat again with her legs pulled up on the bed and brought the scratchy blanket around her to keep the cold at bay.

"Please, Jesus, help my daddy find me," she whispered over and over while rocking back and forth.

FOUR

Day two, 6:30 p.m.: Ashley missing twenty-four hours

Madison looked up from studying the interviews she'd finally been able to conduct during the afternoon and early evening. The nearly empty sheriff's station greeted her visual sweep. Rachel worked at her computer while Deputy Nelson stood at the counter, manning the phones, taking care of any other law enforcement business that occurred.

Madison's gaze zeroed in on J.T.'s office, the blinds on the large picture window that afforded him a view of the whole work area, open. He cradled his chin in his right hand as his stare drilled into his desktop. Even from this distance halfway across the cavernous room she could see the dark circles ringing his eyes and the tired lines that made him look ten years older.

The sound of the front door opening drew Madison's attention reluctantly away from J.T. Emma entered the building with a picnic basket and headed straight for her.

Madison smiled at the reverend's wife. "Is that what I think it is?"

"If you think it's dinner, then yes. Colin called me and said J.T. isn't eating. Do you think you can get him to have something? There's enough for the two of you." Emma glanced over her shoulder. "And you, too, Derek and Rachel."

While Deputy Nelson perked up, straightening away from the counter, Madison shoved her chair back and rose. "I'll do my best. Most of the others are across the street at the café."

Emma flipped the top open. The aromas of warm, freshly baked bread and fried chicken flowed from the basket. "Grace, Kim and I have been busy."

"Kim?"

"Yeah, she helped us. It gave her something to do after we finished with the posters and put them up. She made the coleslaw. She said her dad loves it."

"Good." Madison peeked into the basket, her stomach rumbling. "Your food won't go to waste."

"How's it coming? Anything?" Emma took two hefty-sized paper plates and prepared them for Rachel and Derek.

"I'm sure Colin told you the cadaver search dog didn't find anything."

"Yes. He said something about a K-9 dog finding the other black shoe at Eric Carlton's cabin. Does that mean he took her?"

"I don't think so. I think it's just a little too easy." While Emma lavished another two plates with generous helpings of coleslaw, baked beans, bread and fried chicken, Madison licked her lips in anticipation, not realizing until Colin's wife had shown up how hungry she really was. "After the cadaver search dog scoured the lake area, he went to Carlton's cabin and checked it out. Nothing."

Rachel approached them. "Thankfully some criminals aren't too smart. I never thought of Eric as very bright. He may have Ashley with him."

"True, or someone planted the shoe there." Madison picked up hers and J.T.'s meal. "Hopefully we'll find him soon."

"He may not be far. He grew up here and knows the area well. I could see him hiding in some cave or somthing like that." Rachel lifted her plate and drew in a deep breath of the tantalizing scents. "Mmm, this smells wonderful. Thank you and tell Kim and Grace thanks, too."

"Will do. I'll leave the basket in case you all want seconds."

Derek sauntered over to the desk where the food was. "I'll bring it by later. I promise you there won't be anything left."

Madison made her way toward J.T.'s office. "I second that."

She put one plate down on the top of the file cabinet so she could open his door.

When she stepped inside, he raised his head. He tried to hide the anguish in his gaze, but he couldn't quite wipe the desperation from his look.

"It's okay. You don't have to keep up a front for me." Madison laid the food in front of him, then sat in the chair at his side and scooted up so she could place her plate on his desk. "Emma brought this for us." She wasn't sure how much he was aware of what was going on in the outer office.

"I saw her. I just didn't…" His words came to a shaky halt and he dropped his gaze to the dinner before him. After a long moment, he continued, "I hadn't thought about eating."

"Well, think about it. You've got to eat. Kim helped fix this for you." Madison pulled off a piece of the bread, then popped it into her mouth. "You know I can pass up a slice of pie or cake, but wave bread under my nose and I'm doomed."

A corner of his mouth quirked ever so slightly. "Not me. Sweets any day over breads. I bet Kim made this coleslaw."

"She told Emma you love it."

J.T. stuck his fork in the pile of slaw and brought some to his mouth. "She's right." He slid the utensil between his parted lips.

Madison tore her attention away from him and started on her piece of fried chicken, golden brown, crisp and delicious. She waited until J.T. had taken several bites of his food before asking, "Where do you think we should go next in the investigation?"

He chewed, his forehead wrinkled in thought. "I think the trail that stopped abruptly on the gravel road is where Ashley was taken away. She's not in the woods behind my house or, for that matter, in the lake. She was driven away which means someone might have seen the car and doesn't even know it."

"The car Mrs. Goldsmith saw?"

"A definite possibility. Anything on it?"

The urge to brush a crumb of the fried chicken from the corner of his mouth riveted her attention to his lips. With an effort she remained seated and touched the same area on her face, saying, "You've got something there." While he used his white paper napkin, she shifted her gaze to her food, forcing herself to concentrate on it rather than his mouth. "Not anything yet, but it shouldn't be long with the partial plate number and color."

"By the time we got that it had been half a day. In twelve hours they could be six or seven hundred miles away."

She again looked across the desk at him. "Then I'll make sure the information goes out across the country. So you think we should assume she's been removed from the vicinity?"

"If it's an ex-con I crossed, I can't see him staying around here. If it's Eric, he may still be near. However, Eric doesn't drive a metallic blue car."

"It could be stolen."

"Nothing's been reported stolen."

"Not here but what about somewhere around here like Central City?"

Interest sparked in his eyes. "Yes. We've had a few kids from Central City take cars then ride around before dumping them here at the lake."

"I'll do some checking on stolen cars in the surrounding counties. Maybe Eric drove to Central City, or somewhere like that, took a car and came back and kidnapped Ashley."

J.T. shook his head. "That seems too elaborate for

Eric. It would be more likely he would use his own car and hide somewhere nearby."

"That's what Rachel thinks. She said he could be holed up in some cave around here. How extensive is the cave system in the area?"

"The K-9 dogs from Central City will be back tomorrow to do some checking of places like that where someone can hide. But I don't think that search will yield anything." J.T. finished his coleslaw and put his fork on his plate. "I know Eric is a sex offender, but his victim was a nineteen-year-old female. He was peeping into her house and watching her. Then he went the next step and tried to force himself on her."

"Maybe he's progressed to little girls."

Jaws clenched, J.T. crushed his paper napkin into a tight ball, then tossed it into the trash can by her feet. "I don't think so, but we have to check everything out. Frankly, though, I think this kidnapping is too complicated for someone like Eric."

"Still, until we find him, we won't know anything for sure."

"I've been wrong in the past. With this case I can't be wrong and I can't ignore anything."

The fervent way he said that last sentence reaffirmed her own determination to make sure he was right. Silence fell between them while he folded his paper plate and it followed the napkin into the trash. His jerky movements highlighted the exhaustion she saw in his face.

Glad to see he'd eaten almost half of the chicken and all the slaw and bread, she also threw her empty plate away. "You're convinced it's someone from your past?"

He stabbed her with his sharp gaze. "Yes. A gut feeling, you could say."

Somehow she had to get him to rest and possibly sleep some or she would see him fall apart before her eyes. That thought pierced her heart. "I can start on the list Rachel's drawing up. Why don't you go see your kids and get some rest?"

Anger slashed deep lines into his face. "No. You think I can sleep knowing that Ashley is out there somewhere wondering where I…"

The force of his words died as his sentence came to a halt. She'd known he wasn't ready to admit he needed sleep, but she had to ask. "At least go see Kim and Neil. Kim wanted me to talk to you about assisting with the search. She needs to do something to help. She's hurting."

His eyes narrowed. "I don't need you to tell me that."

"Then go talk to her. Let her help do something."

The fierceness in his expression crumbled. He scrubbed his hands down his face. "I could have lost her, too, yesterday. She was in the house, the back door unlocked. If it is an ex-con, he could go after my whole family before this is over with."

"Not if he's long gone. You, yourself, said it wouldn't be smart for him to hang around here. You're too familiar with the people in your county. It would be hard for him to hide for long."

"But Rachel's right. There are places a person could hide for a while. There's a lot of rough terrain around part of the lake."

"Let Kim breathe, J.T. Let her be a part of finding Ashley. She needs that right now." She didn't normally suggest a fourteen-year-old help with an investigation, but she'd seen the guilt and pain in his daughter's eyes when they had talked earlier that day. "At least keep her informed of what's going on. Maybe she could come down here and answer the phones. It's important that she's around you right now."

After dragging his hands down his face again, he rubbed his eyes. "I know. There needs to be two of me."

"The parent and the sheriff?"

"Yep." He stared out his window into the large outer room. "I feel so torn. What if I can't do it all?"

Surprised at the confession, Madison sat forward in her chair to close some of the space between them. His question, one he would never have uttered in the past, emphasized the exhaustion clinging to him. "I'll be here to help you any way I can. If that means telling you to slow down and take care of yourself, then I'll do that. Whatever it takes."

The corner of his mouth tilted up. "So I'd better not mess with you?"

She gave him one curt nod. "Right."

"Okay, I'll go see Kim and Neil, but I won't be gone long. When we get back, I'd like to go over the list of criminals I've put away who are out of prison. Actually, the list should include everyone I sent to prison whether they are out or not."

"I'll work with Rachel to make sure it's a complete list. She still has a few she's tracking down." Madison rose. "You know you put away quite a lot of criminals in your days on the Chicago police force."

He came to his feet. "Yes, and I believe one's decided

to even the score." He opened the door and stepped to the side to allow her to go first.

When Madison entered the outer room, she saw Ross and Jill Morgan coming into the station. The frowns on the couple's faces alerted her that something was wrong. Although they headed toward Derek behind the counter, Madison made her way toward them while J.T. stopped to talk to Rachel at her computer.

"I wasn't gonna come down here and say anything with all that you're dealing with, but then I got to thinking this might pertain to your case." Ross leaned into the counter, his voice pitched low as though he hated to disturb J.T.

Madison positioned herself next to Derek and faced the young couple who were in their early thirties. "What happened?"

"We found our dog dead this evening. The vet said the dog's been dead probably since early this morning after we left the house." Jill brought a perfectly manicured hand up to smooth her long blond hair behind her left ear. "I don't think it means anything but Ross does."

The dog Kim had heard barking around the time Ashley went missing was dead. Was there a connection between the animal's death and Ashley's kidnapping or was it just a coincidence? "How did he die?" Madison spied J.T. winding his way toward them.

Ross shot his wife a look. "Jill, it could mean something. The vet said he'd been poisoned. I found a half-eaten steak by the fence that I hadn't given Buddy." Dressed still in his business suit, Ross loosened his tie with a frustrated jerk.

"Where's the steak?" J.T. came up to the other side of Madison.

"I left it on the ground while I took my dog to the vet. I'm sorry to bother you with this—" Ross peered again at his wife "—but we remembered you asking if we were home around six yesterday when Buddy was heard barking. There probably isn't any connection to Buddy's death and Ashley's kidnapping, but I didn't want to be the judge of that." Ross's gaze skimmed from J.T. to Madison. "I mean what if our dog saw the kidnapper?"

Her frown deepening, Jill stood a step back from her husband. "I doubt it, Ross."

"I'm glad you came here and reported Buddy's death. You never know what's important and what isn't. This might have something to do with Ashley's disappearance."

When J.T. spoke, Ross refocused on him. "Good. I wanted to help search earlier, but Susan said there were enough searchers, so we went on to work. If there is anything I can do, please let me know."

"Derek, I'd like you to follow Ross home, bag the steak and have a look around the yard. We'll have the lab see what kind of poison was used."

After the deputy and J.T.'s neighbor left, Madison turned to J.T. "You think the dog's poisoning has something to do with Ashley?"

He shrugged. "I'm not ignoring anything unusual happening. It probably doesn't, but we don't have too many pets poisoned in Crystal Springs." J.T. removed his keys from his pocket. "If I'm not back before Derek, have him log the steak in and send it to the lab."

J.T. strode to the door. Madison sagged against the counter. He might not be ready to admit he was tired, but she was. Her eyes burned and her body felt as though she was carrying around an extra twenty pounds. She buried her face in her hands and ground her palms into her eyes.

Father, I need strength and energy to keep going.

She shoved away from the counter and made a detour to the coffeepot. She filled a large mug with the steaming black brew, then crossed the room to Rachel to complete the list of criminals who could possibly hold a grudge against J.T.

Too many from what Rachel had compiled so far. It would take days—days they didn't have—to track down all these people.

Day two, 7:30 p.m.: Ashley missing twenty-five hours

"Daddy!" Kim threw herself into J.T.'s arms the second she saw him in the Fitzpatricks' living room.

He hugged her to him and kissed the top of her head. "I really appreciated the coleslaw."

She leaned back. "I made it because I know how much you like it."

"Well, I ate every last bite of it. Thank you, honey."

The smile that entered his daughter's eyes for a few seconds made this trip worth every minute away from Ashley's investigation. Somehow he had to find his youngest and yet give his other two children the support and comfort they needed.

Lord, please give me the fortitude my family needs.

"Are we going home?"

"Honey, I'll be staying at the station again tonight. I need you to stay with Emma and Colin for one more night."

"But, Daddy, I want to go home."

"I know, baby. But I don't want you there without me and there's too much I need to do right now."

"I want to help. Let me come to the station."

J.T. remembered what Madison had said earlier. "How about tomorrow? I could use you to answer the phones and help Susan out. Will you?"

Her expression brightened. "Yes. Anything. I—I..."

"What?"

Shaking her head, she stepped out of his embrace. "Nothing. It's not important."

"If it's important to you, it's important to me."

Her mouth firmed into a frown. "I said it was nothing."

J.T. started to reassure Kim she hadn't done anything wrong concerning Ashley, but Colin and Neil's appearance in the room stilled his words. He would talk with his daughter in private about what he felt was behind her sudden impudent words and frown.

"You don't look too good, Dad."

"I can always count on you, Neil, to tell it like it is." J.T. peered at his son and saw the same shadows under his eyes and the deep tired lines on his youthful face. They were so much alike it was scary at times. He could recall all the hard knocks he'd experienced in his life and didn't want that for Neil. "You two have got to take care of yourselves. I need you to eat and get some rest."

"Right back at you." Neil folded his arms across his chest and stared at him.

"I will."

"When? I heard you tell Kim you were staying at the station again tonight."

First Madison and now Neil. Didn't they understand the clock was ticking down on this kidnapping? He knew it was because they cared, but he wasn't the important one at the moment. "I have some things I need to organize."

"Can't someone else do it?" Neil moved toward him.

"No! I'm in charge." If he said it enough, maybe then he would believe it because right now he needed to believe he had some control over the situation, that his presence and knowledge in the middle of the case was making a difference.

"I thought that was what the FBI was doing here."

"Yeah, Daddy, we—" Kim caught a look from her brother and clamped her mouth closed.

"The FBI are here at my request, but I'm still the sheriff and in charge." He put a hand on his son's shoulder. "Look, I promise both of you I'll try and sleep on the couch in my office." He didn't tell them he doubted he would get any rest even as tired as he was. He drew his son to him and held both his children, relishing their presence in his arms. If anything happened to them, too, he didn't know what he would do. He couldn't lose them. In his gut he knew the motive for the kidnapping was revenge. He had to find the person targeting his family before something else happened.

"Let's pray for Ashley." J.T. took each of his childrens' hands and bowed his head. "Dear Heavenly Father, we need your strength. Please bring Ashley home safe and sound. Watch over her and protect her from harm. In Jesus Christ's name. Amen."

"I love you." Kim squeezed him around the waist.

"Honey, I love you and Neil. I'll bring Ashley home." When he pulled back, he looked each of them in the eye. "We'll sleep in our own beds tomorrow night, but right now I'd better get back to the station. I have a lot to do tonight."

"Can I help?" Colin crossed the living room.

J.T. caught his gaze. "You're doing it. You're taking care of the most precious things to me."

Emma shouted from the kitchen, "Dinner's ready."

Colin glanced toward the door into the dining room. "Did you have enough food earlier?"

"Yes. Tell your wife and Grace thanks for thinking of me." J.T. kissed Kim on the cheek, patted Neil's arm, then headed toward the entry hall. "I'll call tomorrow morning, Kim, to let you know when you can come down to the station."

"I'm coming, too." Neil stood by his sister.

J.T. gave them a nod then disappeared into the foyer where he paused and drew in a composing breath. He held his hands out in front of him and noticed the tremors. He clenched them into such tight fists that they ached.

He remembered pouring Ashley her cereal yesterday morning. She'd only eaten a few bites before Neil had to leave for school. She'd blown him a kiss as she'd rushed after her brother. Not having fixed himself anything yet for breakfast, he'd just finished hers and downed her untouched orange juice. Was the kidnapper feeding his baby? The thought that maybe she was hungry made his stomach tighten.

"Are you taking care of yourself, J.T.?"

The reverend's question brought his head up, and he spun toward the man framed in the doorway into the living room. He peered behind them to see if Neil or Kim was there.

"They're in the kitchen. I just wanted to make sure you were okay. That you were holding up. I have to admit that your son's right. You don't look well."

"How do you think I should look? I'm living a parent's worst nightmare." J.T. gestured at his face. "So expect it to be reflected in these lines."

"Did the search today produce any evidence to help you?"

"Yes, but not nearly enough. There might be something found on Ashley's clothes, but I'm not holding my breath." Finding his daughter's clothes took J.T. mentally in a whole new direction that at the moment he couldn't handle if he was going to keep himself together.

Colin studied him for a few seconds, opened his mouth to say something but didn't.

"I don't know if you heard or not, but her other shoe was found at Eric's cabin."

"Someone mentioned that to me." Colin moved nearer. "Eric's a troubled individual, but I don't think he took Ashley."

"Were you counseling him?"

"Yes."

Agitated, J.T. took a step toward the reverend. "Do you know anything that could help us?"

Colin shook his head. "I can't tell you what went on in our sessions, but I can assure you I don't know anything that could lead you to Ashley."

Some of the tension siphoned from J.T. He leaned back against the front door. "I don't think he took Ashley, either. Finding the shoe was just too convenient. I think it was planted at his cabin by someone who wants us to believe it's Eric."

"Then where is Eric? Do you think someone harmed him and that's why he isn't around?"

"I don't know. Maybe Eric got frightened by the nature of this case and ran. He was bound to know we would take a close look at him. I do feel whoever took my daughter planned the abduction. This isn't a spur-of-the-moment kidnapping which is what I think Eric would have done."

"And people in prison have a lot of time to plan kidnappings. I heard you were taking a look at criminals you were responsible for putting in jail."

"Yes. I'd better get going. I still have a lot to do tonight. Thanks again for taking care of Neil and Kim. At least I don't have to worry about them when they are with you and Emma."

"We'll do anything we can to help."

J.T. twisted around and grabbed the door handle.

"J.T., that includes listening to you when you need to talk."

He glanced over his shoulder. "I know." He wrenched

the door open and stepped out onto the porch. He was afraid if he started talking to Colin the dam he had built around his emotions would burst and flood him. Then how effective would he be for Ashley, for Neil and Kim who needed him to be strong?

The watcher slid back into the shadows as J.T. exited the reverend's house. Dusk blanketed the landscape and afforded many places to hide.

J.T. paused on the porch and scanned the street. Anguish marked his features and gripped his body in rigid lines.

Yes!

Even from a distance J.T.'s misery could be felt. The watcher chuckled and savored what was to come.

FIVE

Day two, 6:30 a.m.: Ashley missing thirty-six hours

Madison bolted to a sitting position. *Where am I?*

Blinking, she examined her surroundings, her mind groggy from sleep. Boxes were stacked against one wall while an old desk was pushed against the opposite one. A musty smell assaulted her nostrils. She shoved her fingers through her hair, trying to bring some order to the unruly strands.

She remembered now where she was and why. Because J.T. had finally lain down on his couch to rest, she'd decided to catch some sleep in the small storeroom at the back of the sheriff's station instead of the motel where the rest of the FBI agents were staying. Although there were two deputies on the night shift, she hadn't wanted J.T. to be alone in case something happened in the middle of the night.

Madison swung her legs over the side of the uncomfortable cot and rose. She did a series of quick stretches to work the aches out of her body. She felt as though she had gone fifteen rounds with the heavyweight boxing champion and had lost.

A dim light from a window over the desk made patterns across the linoleum floor. Madison checked her watch. Six-thirty in the morning. She'd gotten three hours of sleep in the past two nights. Did J.T. get any?

She left the storeroom, her gaze immediately seeking the individuals in the large outer office. Rachel was at her computer, typing, probably had been there all night. Derek strode into the station, waving at the deputy at the counter. In the far corner a middle-aged woman bent over and picked up a trash can, then emptied it into a large plastic bag a young man about twenty held open for her. She moved on to the next desk and began picking up the used foam cups.

The blinds over the window in J.T.'s office were still pulled shut. Madison crossed to his door and eased it open. In the dark shadows she saw J.T. stretched out on his couch. A snore penetrated the silence. She smiled and started backing away.

J.T. rolled over and his eyes popped open, immediately fastening onto her. "What time is it?" Sleepiness laced his voice.

"Six-thirty."

He shot up. "I've slept too long. Why didn't someone wake me up?"

Madison moved into his office, flipped on the overhead light and closed the door. "I hate to be the one to tell you, but three hours isn't too long."

His head sagged forward while he massaged the back of his neck. "That's your opinion."

She planted her fists on her hips. "And my opinion is the only one that counts in this case. I told everyone not to disturb you."

His head yanked up, a lock of his black hair falling forward from the sudden action. "You did what?"

She dug her fingernails into her palms to keep from smoothing the strand back into place. "I told Kirk to get me if there was any news."

"I am in charge." He surged to his feet, anger erasing all sleepiness from his expression.

"And I would have awakened you if it was warranted. But there must not have been anything happening because I just woke up myself."

A rap at the door cut through the uncomfortable silence that suddenly descended between them.

"Yes." J.T. combed a hand through his short, dark hair.

"Boss, I completed the list of criminals you sent to prison. I highlighted the ones out on parole. It took some doing, but I found out where Neville Sommers is." Rachel held some papers in her fist.

"Where?"

"Mexico. He broke his parole and fled there."

"He hasn't returned to this country?"

Rachel shook her head. "No, he's sitting in a jail in Mexico City. So that's one down and—" she glanced at the sheets "—forty-four to go. I'm happy to report a lot of criminals you put behind bars are still there."

He released a long, protracted breath. "Forty-four. That's forty-three too many. We have our work cut out for us."

"I think we should each take part of the list and start

eliminating ex-cons." Madison took the sheets from Rachel and gave part of them to J.T.

"Have the lab reports come back on Ashley's—" J.T. paused for a few heartbeats "—clothes? The shoes? The steak left at the Morgans'?"

"No. I hope they'll be in later today." Rachel turned to leave.

"You need to go home and get some rest." When Rachel started to protest, he added, "You've been here all night, not to mention the night before." J.T. rounded his desk and plopped down in his chair. "Tell Derek whenever the lab reports come in to get them to me immediately."

"Will do." Rachel closed the door as she exited the office.

Quiet reigned for a few seconds until Madison said, "Before we get started, we should grab some breakfast at the café."

He scanned the first sheet of names. "You go ahead."

She took two steps to his desk and snatched the papers from his grasp. "I don't like eating alone. I do that too much. Besides, I want you to tell me about these felons I'll be tracking down. Over breakfast sounds like a good time to discuss the list."

He glared up at her. "Did anyone ever tell you that you're a bossy—"

She waved her hand, dismissing his words. "All the time. C'mon. We can beat the morning crowd." She didn't give him his part of the names back, but instead, stuck it with hers as she spun around and headed toward his door. When she opened it, the middle-aged woman with gray feathered through her brown hair froze in the action of knocking.

She smiled toward J.T. "Can I clean your office?" She peered inside, wrinkling her nose. "It sure could use it."

"Yeah, I'll be back in a half hour, Elizabeth. Sorry about the mess."

"Don't you worry about it. Ken and I are praying for your little girl."

"Thanks." J.T. stepped out of his office.

Everywhere she went in Crystal Springs people were expressing their concerns and offering J.T. their prayers. He was well loved in the town—except perhaps by one person. J.T. thought it was someone from his past, but she hadn't totally ruled out that it might be someone who lived in the area.

Madison peered over her shoulder and spied J.T. trailing behind her. Then she caught sight of Elizabeth and the young man with her entering J.T.'s office. Madison started to avert her attention when she glimpsed the twenty-something's cowboy boots as he disappeared from view.

Remembering the footprints found in J.T.'s backyard made Madison stop for a few seconds and assess the man with the cleaning lady. Tall, lanky with a pointed chin and long hair tied back with a leather strap. He couldn't have weighed more than a hundred and fifty pounds. The person who made the boot impression had been estimated at a hundred eighty. Still, she couldn't rule anyone or anything out. Too much depended on them wading through the evidence and deciding what was relevant and what wasn't. One mistake could cost Ashley her life.

Madison continued forward and waited just outside the door to the station for J.T. The cool early morning air hit her and she pulled her jacket across her front. The scent of baking bread and frying bacon wafted to Madison. Her stomach churned.

J.T. opened the door and joined her on the sidewalk. He glanced up and down the street, as though appraising the area around him. "You know there has been a time or two lately I felt I was being watched." He shrugged and started for the café directly across the road. "I'm sure it's just the thought that whoever took Ashley might want to see what effect it's having on me."

"Who is that young man with Elizabeth?" Madison hurried to keep up with J.T.'s long strides.

"Her oldest son, Ken. Her youngest one is a friend of Neil's."

"What do you know about them?"

He halted on the curb in front of the café and pivoted toward her. "Why the questions?"

"Ken was wearing cowboy boots."

"There are quite a few people around here who do. My son's baseball coach only wears cowboy boots. He says it's a constant reminder of where he's from, Texas. I can't bring in everyone who wears them."

"I'm not suggesting you do. It was just an observation. We can't rule out that the kidnapper might be someone from around here."

"I'm not ruling anyone out. I'm focusing my investigation on the most likely suspects. Right now those are the felons who threatened me."

While he held open the door to the restaurant, Madison entered and the conversation among the few customers ceased when they saw J.T. As they passed the tables to grab one in the back away from the traffic, a couple of people told J.T. how sorry they were for what happened. He nodded and kept going. Madison noticed another man with a pair of cowboy boots and decided J.T. was probably right—for the time being. But she filed the bit of information away to be pulled out later if necessary.

Seated at a table for four, J.T. flipped the menu over to the breakfast side and kept his gaze glued to the piece of laminated beige paper. Madison studied hers, and when the waitress came over she ordered a ham omelet with whole wheat toast.

The young woman looked up from her pad. "J.T., do you want your usual?"

J.T. didn't say anything. Madison wondered if he'd even heard the waitress. Madison reached across the table and touched his arm. She felt the bunched muscles beneath her fingertips. She gently shook him. "J.T., you need to order."

He peered at the waitress, a blank expression on his face for a couple of seconds before he said, "I want my usual."

After the waitress departed, Madison took their menus and put them behind the napkin holder. "I didn't get to ask you last night. How did your visit with Kim and Neil go?"

"As well as can be expected, I guess. Kim wants to go home. I told them we would tonight."

"Probably not a bad idea. They need familiar surroundings."

"I promised Kim she could come down and answer the phones today. Neil, too."

"I can understand them wanting to help."

"I don't want them down at the station. I don't…" He closed his eyes.

Without really thinking what she was doing, Madison cupped his hand. "Are you afraid you won't be able to keep up the facade?"

His gaze jerked to hers. "Yes! I know how scared they are, and if they see how scared I am, it won't be good."

"It's okay to be human. Have you prayed together as a family?"

"Not nearly enough."

"Then do. That might help Neil and Kim. You, too."

When J.T.'s gaze lowered to her hand holding his, an urge to slip hers away warred with her need to comfort him. Being a friend won. "They have some strong emotions they're trying to deal with. You might need to show them you're dealing with the same ones."

"Lead by example."

"From what your staff tells me, you're very good at that. The same goes in a family."

The waitress brought their food, placing their hot plates in front of them. J.T.'s usual turned out to be pancakes and eggs. He slathered butter on the pancakes then drenched them in maple syrup.

"I'm glad you got your appetite back." When he gave her a quizzical look, she gestured toward his plate.

He looked down. "Not really. I just didn't want to think about what to order. One less decision to make."

"Let's eat and discuss the names on the list."

J.T. pushed his plate to the side and reached for his sheets.

Madison snatched them up before he could and put the whole list on the chair next to her. "Eat. Then we'll talk."

He scowled but cut into the stack of pancakes.

Halfway through her omelet, Madison wiped her mouth, then sipped her coffee, cradling the mug between her palms. "I want you to think about the list of people you've put away. Who are the top five who might do something like kidnap your daughter?"

He chewed the last of the eggs, staring beyond her shoulder into space. "I would have said Neville Sommers would be at the top of the list, but we know he wasn't involved so…" His voice faded, his shoulders lifting in a shrug.

"I'm going to call Mexico City and check to make sure the information is correct."

"That's not a bad idea. There might have been a time he was in jail in Mexico, but maybe he's out and back in this country. I don't want to miss any likely suspects." With his pancakes half eaten, J.T. shoved his food away.

"We won't. So who else?"

"Let's see. Timothy Connors would be on the list definitely. He actually came at me in court. He was dragged out in chains. Then there is Willie Hayes. I won't repeat what he told me he would do to me and my family. Chris Kline is a cold one. He didn't have to say much. His body language said it all."

Madison picked up the sheets and began scanning for the names. "I see Connors's name on here. He's out. But Hayes is still in jail and Kline is dead."

"Dead? When?"

"About three years ago in a prison fight."

"That doesn't surprise me. Underneath all that icy veneer, he was a mean one. Where is Connors?"

"He checks in with his parole officer in Chicago."

"Just two hours away." A nerve in J.T.'s jaw jerked. "He'll be the first person I check into."

"Okay. Give me some more names."

"Let me look at the list."

She shook her head. "I want your gut feeling before you go through the names on the list. Who stands out the most in your memory?"

"Okay." J.T. held his coffee up, his elbows on the table, and drank. "Another one is Aaron Adam Acker. I dubbed him the Triple A Man. He had a mean streak a mile wide. Explosive temper." He snapped his fingers. "Then there is Joe Washington." He paused for half a minute. "He liked girls—all ages."

Madison checked the list again. "Acker is out. Has been for almost a year. He reports to his parole officer in St. Louis."

"That's farther away, but he could get here in under half a day. How about Washington?"

"Still in prison. He started a fight and murdered an inmate so he'll be there for quite a while."

J.T. blew out a long sigh. "Good."

"Anyone else come to mind?"

J.T. finished the last dregs of his coffee. "No. Wait. There is another one. Bobby Johnson. I almost forgot about his threats."

"Why? They weren't that serious?"

"No, they were." He pressed his lips together, running his finger around the rim of his mug. Looking away, he shifted in his chair. "I went to court drunk. I'm not sure I remembered very well that time in my life. A lot of things are fuzzy."

Drunk? Stunned by his admission, Madison couldn't think of anything to say for a long moment. An uncomfortable silence hung between them. "Then are you sure?" she asked finally, trying to recall if she had ever seen him take a drink the year before. No, never.

"Yes. His description of my slow death is memorable even through an alcoholic haze." He pinned her beneath his intense regard. "I'm a recovering alcoholic, Madison, have been for almost six years. That time in my life isn't something I'm proud of." He hoped he never returned to that life, but he couldn't let down his guard—ever.

She still didn't know what to think of J.T.'s confession. She couldn't afford at the moment to let it sidetrack her. Veiling her expression, Madison ran her gaze down the first page then the second until she found Bobby Johnson. "He was just paroled two months ago and he's living outside of Chicago about an hour and a half away from here."

J.T. sucked in a gulp of air. "Then he goes up at the top with Connors. Both men are a great place to start our investigation."

After the waitress took their breakfast plates away then refilled their mugs, Madison came around to the chair next to J.T. Her nearness threw him off-kilter for a few seconds. Her scent of apples and cinnamon vied with the aromas in the café, and all he could focus on was the last time he had a piece of apple pie at the Fourth of July church picnic with his family.

"Now let's go through the list and prioritize the people on it."

He heard Madison speaking as if through a long tunnel. He couldn't believe her presence suddenly had such an effect on him. She was a friend—a good friend—but that was all he could emotionally handle right now. He forced himself to concentrate on the paper in front of him.

"Mark one if we need to immediately look into them, two if we can wait a day or so and three if they're probably not a threat so we can wait until everyone else is cleared." She spread out the sheets on the table. "I've already highlighted the people you named. Those will be first before anyone else. If you can remember their threats after all this time, then we have to take them very seriously."

As he penciled a number by the names, his gaze trekked down the full length of each piece of paper—all six of them. He had been directly responsible for putting these people behind bars doing hard time. Maybe he should have seen this list years ago when he'd thought nothing he had done had helped stem the tide of criminals on the street. Maybe he wouldn't have started drinking.

But because of his job, Ashley was in jeopardy. Guilt pummeled him from all sides. How was he going to live with it if something happened to his daughter? His wife's death had sent him completely over the edge he had been teetering on for a year with his drinking.

Six years ago he hadn't known the Lord. He wasn't alone as before.

"Rachel, put the names of the ones out on parole in bold letters so it's easy to pick them out." Madison pointed to the first person on the list.

Although he heard her words, their meaning didn't register for an extra few seconds. All he saw was the fact there were forty-four felons out that had a grudge against him. The thought sent a shudder down his spine.

Too many. Not enough time.

"J.T.?"

He compelled himself to fasten his full attention on Madison, on the case. He was thankful she was here to help him. "Ready to go back. There's a lot to do."

She nodded. A frown creased her forehead and worry dulled her eyes.

He rose. The sound of the chair scraping against the tile floor grated on his raw nerves. As he headed across the street to the sheriff's office, all he could think about was: too many felons, not enough time.

Day two, 11:30 a.m.: Ashley missing forty-one hours

"Someone brought homemade sugar cookies and put them in the break room." Susan stopped by the table where Madison worked at one end and Kim at the other, answering phones and logging the calls.

Kim perked up. "Mrs. Goldsmith's?"

"Yeah, how did you know?"

"She makes the best ones I've ever had." Kim stood. "When she makes a batch, she always shares some with us. Ashley loves…" A thickness rose in the teenager's voice, a sheen glazed her eyes.

"I could sure use a few right about now." Madison pushed back from the computer she had been sitting in front of for the past few hours. "I think my eyes have crossed." She made a face as though her eyes really had.

A smile leaked into Kim's sad expression. "I'll get you a couple. There's some soft drinks. Do you want one?"

Madison held up her mug, half full of lukewarm black coffee. "I'll stick with this. Thanks."

Susan's gaze followed Kim's progress toward the break room. "Do you think she should be here?" She swung her attention back to Madison. "Don't get me wrong. I have appreciated the help with the phones. They have been ringing off the walls, and with all that needs to be done she's been a big help, but she's really taking this hard."

Madison came to her feet to stretch and work the kinks out of her muscles produced from sitting in the same hard chair for hours. "As to be expected. She needs to help. This seemed the best way. We're here if she needs help dealing. More importantly J.T. is." She looked toward the break room. "Hopefully when they return to their house tonight, things will be better. Being away from familiar surroundings can add to the stress for everyone involved."

"Not just Kim?"

"No, J.T., too. He's been camped here since the kidnapping. I think spending some time at his home with his family will be good for him."

"Among familiar surroundings?"

"Yes." Madison twisted from side to side.

"Won't that spark memories of Ashley that would make it harder for him?"

The quick stretches eased the aches enough for Madison to sit again. "Maybe. I'm no psychologist, but I think it will help in the long run for the whole family." Peering beyond the older woman, Madison glimpsed Kim emerging from the break room with a paper plate full of cookies and a soft drink. "Thanks, Susan, for letting us know about these."

"I'm going to go across the street to the café to get some food in an hour. I'm taking orders. Do you want anything?"

"Why don't you bring a turkey sandwich for me and one for J.T.? Knowing him, he'll probably not take the time to eat lunch."

"Will do."

Kim placed cookies in the middle of the table. "I already had one. They're great!"

Susan shuffled toward Rachel and an FBI colleague, Paul Kendall, both situated before another computer working on the list of criminals. With a quick scan around the large room, Madison noted the price this abduction had exacted from the various members of J.T.'s team. Tired lines aged Susan's face and worry painted her complexion a pasty white. Dark smudges circled Rachel's eyes, dulled to a lackluster brown. None of Derek's usual cockiness was evident now and Kirk ran on cup after cup of coffee, which made his movements jerky.

Madison glanced down at her own hands poised over the keyboard. Their slight tremor brought a smile to her lips. Obviously not just J.T.'s team was affected. Hours ago coffee probably replaced the blood coursing through her veins.

Before getting back to her task of checking the criminal list, Madison grabbed a cookie off the paper plate and took a bite. The delicious sweetness melted in her mouth. She finished that one and got another.

"I probably should warn you that Mrs. Goldsmith's cookies are addicting." Kim snagged one for herself as the phone rang.

While the teenager answered it, Madison munched and thought about what J.T. had revealed this morning over breakfast. He was a recovering alcoholic. Having witnessed his strong personality and control, she was surprised by his revelation. As she finished a third cookie, she again surveyed the people in the room. What were they hiding? The realization that others often hid behind a mask like a clown strengthened her earlier idea. She still couldn't rid her mind of the thought the kidnapper could be someone J.T. knew.

When J.T. emerged from his office with Matthew, he came over to Madison. "I just got off the phone with the lab in Central City. There weren't any useful leads derived from Ashley's clothing. The poison used on the Morgan's dog was boric acid."

"Is it common?"

"It can be found in a medicine cabinet as an antiseptic. I'll have Derek do some checking around to see if any has been purchased lately, but if the kidnapper poisoned the Morgans' dog, you can bet he didn't buy it nearby."

"If the kidnapper took Ashley out by the gravel road, he had to go right by the Morgans' yard."

"Buddy liked to bark at anyone who came around his place. It often drove the neighbors crazy." J.T. sat on the corner of the desk, folded his arms over his chest. "So the dog was probably barking at the exact time of the abduction which means six o'clock."

Madison walked to the dry erase board and wrote the dog's poisoning on it as well as when it was barking. She noticed the metallic blue car that Mrs. Goldsmith had seen pulling out of the side street near the gravel road had been at five-forty. The timeframe didn't quite jell, but it was still a lead that needed to be tracked down. "Now if only we could find this car and who was driving it."

"Since one that fits the description has been reported missing in Central City, it might turn up soon."

"Or it's being sold for spare parts as we speak."

Inky blackness pressed in on Ashley. Her body curled into a tight ball, she huddled under the itchy blanket on the cot. Warmth evaded her. A chill that always hung in the air caused her teeth to chatter.

Where was Daddy? Why hadn't he come?

She didn't like the bad man. She'd tried to be good so he would leave the light on, but he always turned it off after she'd eaten. She wanted to tell him she would be good, but she never saw him. The last time when a peanut butter and jelly sandwich had been delivered, she'd shouted the words near the doggy door, hoping he would hear her, right after she had started eating her food. He'd switched off the light a couple of seconds later.

With the sandwich clutched in her hand, she'd stumbled down the stairs and missed the bottom one. The pain in her ankle still hurt. Ashley rubbed it. Tears filled her eyes.

Hunger pangs competed with her throbbing ankle for her attention. The bad man had been gone a long time. What if he had left?

For a moment relief at the thought that he might be gone pushed her to a sitting position. Then fear of being left alone forever drove all joy from her. Tears slid down her face and fell onto her lap.

"Daddy, where are you?"

Day two, 1:00 p.m.: Ashley missing forty-two and a half hours

"Dad, Kim and I are going with Emma and Colin to put up posters in Central City."

J.T. lifted his head and stared at his son in the doorway into his office. "I thought Kim wanted to help down here?"

Neil gestured toward his sister. "I don't think she counted on it being so hard on her. She wouldn't say anything to you, but she's getting more withdrawn as the day passes. She's not even answering the phone anymore. She's sitting in the break room, staring at the floor."

J.T. surged to his feet, nearly toppling his chair in his haste. "Why didn't you say something earlier?" He should have realized Kim wasn't handling this well. But he'd been holed up in his office making calls to parole officers and police trying to get information on the people he'd put behind bars. Rachel, Paul, Madison and himself had finally narrowed the list down to eight ex-cons, a much more manageable number.

He crossed the large outer room and entered the back one used for breaks. The sight of Kim sitting on the small couch, her shoulders hunched, her head sagging forward, her hands twisting together, over and over, ripped a hole through his heart as though a bullet had pierced it.

He took the empty seat next to Kim and pulled her into his arms. "Honey, you've been such a big help today. Just having you here has helped me."

"But we haven't been able to find Ashley." Kim buried her face into his shoulder, her arms about him.

He stroked her back and held her tight.

"I don't know what else to do."

"We'll go to prayer service for Ashley tonight. Colin plans to have one every evening until Ashley is home safely. We can't have too many prayers. Until then go with Neil, Emma and Colin to Central City. You can put up some more posters. You never know when someone might see your poster and come forward with the piece of information we need to find Ashley."

Kim leaned back, her eyes red, her face ghostly white. "You'll be all right until we get back?"

"So long as you're with Colin, Emma and Neil, I'll be okay. Promise me you won't go anywhere by yourself until this is all over."

She nodded solemnly.

He didn't want to scare Kim, but he didn't want her to be by herself until he knew where the threat to his family was coming from and had taken care of it.

"Let's pray." J.T. held both her hands. "Lord, we need Your guidance. Show us what to do to find Ashley. Be a shield around her and protect her from any harm. Amen."

"Daddy, I didn't mean for this to happen."

He framed her face, smoothing his hands through her hair. "Of course, you didn't."

The tears returned to fill Kim's eyes. "But you don't understand. The other day I wished I didn't have a sister. She was always following…" His daughter, with wet tracks streaking her cheeks, plastered herself against his chest and cried.

J.T. closed his eyes. Her sobs wrenched him. He let her cry for a few minutes because it was important for her to release the emotions she'd been wrestling with the past two days. But it was one of the hardest things he had done to listen to his child pour out her agony. Each tear was like acid eroding his own composure.

When Kim quieted, J.T. prayed for guidance, then pulled back and looked her in the eye. "You didn't wish this to happen. You aren't to blame. I'll bring Ashley back."

"How, Daddy?"

He took her face between his hands and made sure he had her full attention. "Don't you worry about that. Just know I will."

Madison came to a halt inside the room. A movement out of the corner of his eye caused J.T. to whip around. "The kidnapper is on the phone. You've got fifteen seconds to answer or he hangs up."

SIX

Day two, 1:00 p.m.: Ashley missing forty-two and a half hours

J.T. hurried to the nearest phone in the large outer room.

"Line one." Madison stood to his side.

"Put a trace on this call." J.T. lifted the receiver, his hand tight about the cold plastic to keep it from trembling.

"We're on it." Madison placed a pad and pencil on the desk.

Although the call would be recorded, J.T. appreciated the paper in case he wanted to take notes. Phone to ear, he said, "J. T. Logan here."

There was a pause of several seconds, then a mechanical voice, rough, deep sounding, came across the wire. "I'll say this one time only. I want a hundred thousand dollars in small bills in exchange for your daughter. I'll call you again in a couple of hours to tell you where to bring it. Just in case you've forgotten what's at stake here. Listen."

J.T.'s grip tightened even more.

Then he heard his youngest daughter's voice. "Daddy, where are you?"

Click.

"No!" The connection ended before he could say anything to Ashley. His baby had been only a phone call away.

His numbed fingers opened, and the receiver crashed to the desktop. Ashley's anguish-filled words echoed through his mind. He would never forget them or the fear that vibrated through each word. He leaned into the desk to keep himself upright. His fingers dug into its wooden edge as he tried to bring his emotions under control enough to speak.

"Did we get a location?" Madison asked for him.

Rachel stood up from her computer. "He used a landline. We didn't have enough time. The only thing we got was the call was made from somewhere in Crystal Springs."

"He's here," J.T. whispered, and lowered his head for a few seconds while he fought the overwhelming anger that seized him. "Ashley's here."

"Maybe. Ashley's voice could have been recorded. She might not be with the man. He may be here only long enough to get his money and then be gone. What are you going to do about the money?"

Madison's question forced him to quash all the emotions that would stand in his way of doing his job. J.T. straightened and faced her, reassured by her calm tone and serene expression. "Find it somehow. I'll start with the bank."

Kim moved toward him. "What did the kidnapper say, Daddy?"

J.T. glanced back at his daughter, her eyes large, her face so white he was afraid she would faint. This was why she shouldn't be down here. He wanted to shelter her as much as possible, but it was too late. "He wants a hundred thousand dollars."

"A hundred thousand!"

He rounded on Kim, grasped her shoulders and brought her close, hoping to convince her Ashley would be all right and praying he was right. "This is a good thing. He's opening up a dialogue with us. If he's motivated by money, it might be easier to get Ashley back. And because he called, we know he's somewhere in the area, not several states away."

"Yes, but do we have that kind of money?" Kim tightened her arms about J.T.

"Honey, you don't need to worry about that."

As the front door opened and Susan entered with several sacks of food from the café, Neil stepped forward. "Can I do anything?"

J.T. gave a shake of his head, then turned to Madison. "Will you take the kids to Emma and Colin's? When Kirk comes in, I'll send him over to relieve you." He trusted his deputies and Madison to keep his children safe, and right now that was paramount to him if he was going to do his job.

"Yes, of course."

"Dad, I've got my car."

"With the kidnapper so close I would prefer someone with you." When Neil started to say something more, J.T. continued, "Please, son. I don't want to have to worry about you and Kim while I'm trying to put together the money."

Neil nodded once, a frown on his face.

J.T. took hold of Kim's shoulders again and kneaded them. "Honey, I'm afraid you'll have to spend another night at the Fitzpatricks'. I'm sorry, but I'll have to be here until the ransom has been dropped off, until—" the last words lumped together in his throat and he couldn't get them out "—until Ashley is released." He couldn't think of what would happen if she wasn't. This was his chance to get his daughter back.

"I'll get my things." Kim's shoulders sagged.

"I'll let you and your brother know as soon as I find out anything." J.T. peered at Kim until she gave a slight nod in acknowledgment.

While his daughter went back into the break room for her purse and iPod, Madison closed the space between her and J.T. "How long do you think it will be before Kirk returns?"

"Maybe an hour or so. He went to Central City to check out that abandoned car. It might be the one Mrs. Goldsmith saw leaving the area. Right now we need every clue we can get. Let's hope it pans out." He moved into her personal space and lowered his voice. "I have to know my children are safe. With you I do. I know you want to be in the middle of the ransom drop, but I trust you and Kirk to take care of Kim and Neil. He's been with me almost from the beginning, he and Ted."

She gave him a half smile. "You don't need to worry about them. Concentrate on getting the money put together. I'll return to help when Kirk gets to your house." She laid her hand on his arm. "Kim and Neil will be fine."

With Madison's reassurances J.T. realized his children would be okay. As he watched her gather up her purse and wait for Kim, he thanked God for her presence these past two days. She had kept him sane in an insane situation.

Confusion in her expression, Susan approached. "What happened?"

"There's been a ransom demand." J.T. looked toward the break room.

"How much, boss?" Susan laid several sacks on the desk and gave one to Madison.

"A hundred thousand." J.T. watched his daughter trudge toward him.

His secretary whistled. "I have a couple of hundred dollars. You can have it."

Madison turned toward him while Kim and Neil walked toward the front door. "I have some money saved, too. Just let me know. It's not much, but it's a few thousand."

"Thanks, you two, but let me see what I can come up with first."

A hundred thousand! The equity in his house wasn't nearly that much. He didn't know how he was going to come up with the amount in such a short time. But if he had to, he would go door-to-door asking for donations.

Lord, help me!

Day two, 3:30 p.m.: Ashley missing forty-five hours

"A hundred thousand dollars!" Emma picked up her glass of iced tea and came to the table. "Does J.T. have that kind of money?"

Madison slid her gaze toward the doorway, not wanting Kim or Neil to hear. The kids were in the den with Emma and Colin's twin teenage daughters, making more posters while Madison was talking with Emma about how Kim and Neil were holding up. "I don't think so. I called a few minutes ago and Matthew said J.T. hadn't gotten all the money together yet."

After putting her drink on the table, Emma crossed the room to the desk, picked up the phone and dialed. "Dad, I don't know if you've heard but J. T. Logan's little girl was kidnapped the day before yesterday."

Madison remembered meeting Emma's father last year. He was a wealthy businessman who lived in Chicago.

"Yes, it has been hard on everyone. J.T. finally received a ransom demand today for a hundred thousand dollars and—" Emma stopped in midsentence, her eyebrows slashing downward as she listened to what her father said. Suddenly her expression changed to a full-fledged smile. "I knew I could count on you, Dad. J.T. will appreciate it as will everyone in Crystal Springs. Thanks."

Emma swung her attention to Madison. "Dad's donating the money for the ransom. I'll let J.T. know so he doesn't have to worry about that. He has enough on his mind at the moment." She pressed the button on her phone to disconnect her call to her father then punched in another number. "This is Emma. I need to speak to J.T."

Silence filled the kitchen while Madison suspected someone was getting J.T. She tuned out Emma and thought about the fact there was a ransom demand made almost two days after Ashley disappeared. That was unusual. Why so late? Had the kidnapper taken Ashley somewhere else and then come back here? Was the child alive? Abandoned? Maybe the abductor killed Ashley so he was trying to get something out of it since he no longer had the little girl. She hated the direction her thoughts were taking her, but these questions needed to be considered, even proposed to J.T.

When Emma hung up, a smile graced her lips. "At least I could help J.T. in one area."

Madison glanced down at her watch. "The kidnapper should be calling back soon."

"And you want to be there when he does."

Although it wasn't a question, Madison answered, "Yes. I'm flattered J.T. wants me guarding Neil and Kim, but I want to be there for…" Suddenly she realized what she was admitting by saying, "for him."

She cared more than a colleague should. Three years ago she had been engaged and at the church for her wedding when she'd discovered her fiancé had gotten cold feet and called off their wedding. In the end he hadn't been able to accept the profession she had dedicated her life to and he'd known he wouldn't be able to change her mind about being a police officer. At least she hadn't been standing at the altar when he had backed out of getting married, but she could still remember facing her guests and telling them she wasn't going to become Mrs. Brent Harrison that day. In that moment when the pain of rejection had overwhelmed her, she had decided it was best to go through life alone. Now her feelings for J.T. were making her question that decision.

Kim entered the kitchen. Confusion clouded her expression.

How much had Kim overheard of her conversation with Emma? "Did you get a lot of posters made?"

Kim shrugged. "I suppose so." Just inside the doorway, she surveyed the room. Her teeth dug into her lower lip. "What if Dad can't pay the ransom?"

Emma took a sip from her tea. "That won't be a problem. My father is donating the money."

"I've seen shows on TV where the kidnappers warn the people about bringing in the police."

"Kinda hard to do that since your dad is the sheriff." Madison rose. She knew the direction Kim's thoughts were taking and hoped to put a stop to them. "The kidnapper didn't say anything about not bringing in the police or FBI."

"Why not? That seems strange."

"Not everything is like on TV." Madison walked toward Kim, not wanting to get into all the odd aspects of the case.

Emotions flickered across the teen's face. First puzzlement, then doubt before resignation settled on her features. "I guess you're right. I still think it's odd, though."

"Maybe he's challenging us." Emma sat again at the table. "Some criminals like to do that because they think they're better, smarter than the police and the FBI."

To Madison the whole case had a strange feel to it. She couldn't quite figure out what bothered her, but she would. It was too important not to.

The doorbell chimes penetrated the silence.

"I'll get it," Grace called from the hallway.

Madison heard a male voice, then a few seconds later Kirk appeared in the doorway. Relieved to see him, she snatched up her purse, but before taking her leave, she stopped in front of Kim. "Your dad knows what he's doing. I've worked with many police and sheriff departments, and this one is run efficiently because of J.T. which gives us a good chance of getting Ashley back safely."

The teenager crossed her arms and dropped her gaze away. "I know."

But Kim's body language negated her words, and Madison wasn't sure what else to say to the teen to alleviate her guilt and doubts. Only Ashley's return would do that. Maybe the ransom would work. Sometimes it did.

Father, please let this be over soon. I don't know how much more J.T. and his family can take.

In the living room Madison pulled Kirk to the side. "What about the car?"

"It had to be the car Mrs. Goldsmith described. The partial license plate number matches and it's metallic blue. The Central City police have dusted for fingerprints but so far haven't found any matches other than the owners'. It was abandoned in a field outside of town with the CD player gone as well as a case of CDs. There isn't much else. No one saw anything in the area. The nearest house was half a mile away."

"No evidence that Ashley was in the car?"

"None the police found. There are some unknown fingerprints inside. They just aren't in the database."

"Thanks. Maybe something will turn up later."

Anxious to get to the sheriff's office, Madison hurried toward the foyer. Neil stood next to Grace near the front door. His solemn eyes—eyes that reminded her of J.T.'s—connected with hers.

"Please let us know what's going on. The hardest part of all this is not knowing."

"Neil, I'll call when I have some news. I promise."

As the door closed behind her, Madison hugged her arms to her, a tremor rippling down her body. Bright sunlight contradicted the mood of the town. A pall hung over Crystal Springs.

As she made her way to her car, a bird trilled in a nearby oak, lush with green leaves. Last year she had admired the cleanliness and well-kept feel of Crystal Springs. She'd even thought it would be a nice place to retire one day. Scanning the landscape, she saw the same tidy lawns, recently painted houses and beds teeming with flowers. Nothing had changed, and yet everything had.

An evil presence had invaded Crystal Springs. Quaking, she slipped behind her steering wheel. For a second she thought of switching on the heater even though the temperature outside was in the low seventies. Coldness embedded deep in her bones as though the wickedness wrapped itself around her.

Day three, 10:30 p.m.: Ashley missing fifty-two hours

Blackness shrouded the terrain before J.T. He focused on the pain shooting down his back from the tightly corded muscles in his neck and shoulders. Anything to take his mind off his mounting doubt—and fear this wouldn't work.

He hefted the duffel bag from the backseat of his Jeep. The sound of his car door slamming closed echoed through the eerie quiet. He couldn't even hear the water lapping against the shore ten yards away because the night was so motionless. There was not a wisp of a breeze, as if everything had come to a standstill and was waiting.

The hairs on his nape stood up. He was being watched by the Feds, but who else? This whole setup didn't feel right. After receiving the second call from the kidnapper, they'd had hours to stake out the drop-off point. It was pitch black out here now, but something else was going on, he was sure of it.

At least Neil and Kim were being guarded not only by Kirk but also Rachel at the Fitzpatricks'. So if this had been a ploy to get to his other children, it wasn't going to work.

A cloud slithered across the half-moon. J.T. switched on his flashlight. With no town lights nearby on this remote part of the lake, he carefully picked his way toward the shoreline. Something caught his boot and he stumbled forward. Catching himself, he directed the beam of light at his feet, his fear rising to lodge in his throat. A large root stuck out of the ground. Relief washed over him and his rigid stance sagged for a few seconds. He stepped over the obstacle and continued to move forward.

At the edge of the lake J.T. stared out over the water. His flashlight illuminated its smooth surface near him. He knew one team of agents was out on the lake nearby in case the kidnapper came by boat while the other two were on land. In addition to those teams, there were more at a distance, forming a wide perimeter around this location on the water and land.

As instructed, J.T. plopped the bag at the foot of a large pine three feet from the water, then began to retrace his steps to his Jeep. The kidnapper hadn't said anything about not bringing in the police, but he had made it clear that if he didn't get the money and get back to Ashley, she would die. That was why he had insisted that the Feds not touch the man when he took the bag of money. They were hidden well. Would it work? Could they track the kidnapper to where Ashley was being held—if the man even returned to her?

The hardest thing he had to do in all this was to drive away and not stay to see what happened, not to be involved in the stakeout. He had made Madison promise to call him immediately with any news while he sat at his office, as per the kidnapper's instructions to him. As he pulled onto the highway leading into town, he wanted so badly to double back, but if the kidnapper was watching him, that could cost Ashley her life. He kept his Jeep pointed toward Crystal Springs. His hands gripped the steering wheel so tightly they hurt, intensifying the pain and leaving a burning trail down his back.

Day three, 1:30 a.m.: Ashley missing fifty-five hours

Her muscles locked in place, Madison maneuvered to ease the ache in her legs from squatting for hours. Her arms felt as though they weighed a ton from holding up the night-vision binoculars. A thicket of brush surrounded her. The scent of damp vegetation tickled her nose and several times she'd had to catch herself before sneezing because of the moldy odor.

"There's movement out on the water. A boat." A voice came through her earpiece. She swung the binoculars over the lake, visible from her vantage point. In the distance a craft came toward the shore at a fast speed. Suddenly when it was only twenty or so feet away, the boat veered to the right and made a tight U-turn.

"We've been spotted. Do you want us to follow the boat?"

"Stay put. I'll radio the others around the lake to pick up the boat and follow it at a distance. It could be a trick," Matthew Hendricks answered the two agents on the water.

She swung her binoculars to the base of the pine tree. The bag of money was still there. The roar of the speedboat's engine faded in the distance. One of the teams patrolling the perimeter of the lake would pick up the craft and discover where it was headed. Until they heard back, they had to stay and stake out the money.

Again Madison moved to make herself more comfortable. A limb stuck into her back. She scooted forward away from the pointy branch. It was going to be a *long* night.

Day three, 4:30 a.m.: Ashley missing fifty-eight hours

J.T. slammed down the phone. The kidnapper got spooked, and the money was still sitting in the bag on the beach under the tree six hours after he'd made the drop.

He pressed the heels of his hands into his eyes, then rubbed them down his face. Ashley was doomed.

They couldn't even find a trace of the speedboat that was used. Gone. Vanished into thin air, just like Ashley. He realized there were miles and miles of shoreline, but still the FBI had enough teams to cover the area.

What had gone wrong?

He'd taken a risk with his daughter's life, and he'd lost.

With elbows on his desk, J.T. buried his face in his hands, his eyes burning from another night without any rest. He didn't know if he would ever really get a good night's sleep again. Every time he closed his eyes he saw Ashley's face and heard her last words to him.

Daddy, where are you?

He collapsed back in his chair. Instead of being stuck here waiting, he should have been out there. Then maybe they would have found the speedboat. He knew the area better than most.

Drop off the money, leave immediately and go back to your office to wait for my call to tell you where Ashley is. He'd never forget the kidnapper's last instructions before cutting the connection. He'd done what he was supposed to do, and yet no Ashley.

Lord, where are You?

Suddenly for the first time in six years the urge to find a store and buy any kind of alcoholic beverage he could get inundated him. He fished the keys to his Jeep out of his front pocket. The hand that held them quivered. He curled it into a fist and brought it to his lap.

Drinking wouldn't bring Ashley back. It would only dull the pain temporarily. He'd found that out the hard way six years ago.

Once an alcoholic, always an alcoholic.

He could still remember those words being shouted at him by his wife, Lindsay, not hours before she was hit by a car while walking off her anger at him. The police had never found who had struck her, but even if they had, he couldn't have blamed that person for his wife's death. Not really. The guilt was his. She'd been out walking after dark, so angry she probably wasn't even paying attention to her surroundings. And he was the one who had made her that angry.

When Lindsay had been killed, he'd thought he had hit rock bottom. But he hadn't. He'd still had a ways to go in order to begin the climb up out of the abyss he was in. It had taken waking up one day in an alley, beaten, unable to remember how he had even gotten there to realize he had a problem. Thankfully he had hired an excellent live-in housekeeper to watch his children because what had started out as an occasional drink had become an addiction for him. All he had craved was alcohol to the exclusion of his work and family.

J.T. stuffed the keys back in his front pocket. No, he couldn't fall apart right now. Ashley was still alive—she had to be—and needed him to find her.

A soft rap at his door brought him around. "Come in."

Madison entered his office, tiny lines of exhaustion feathering outward from her blue eyes, flat from lack of sleep. "Matthew ordered me to get some rest. Of course, that's nearly impossible with all that happened. He left half the teams in place, but he figures with dawn approaching the kidnapper isn't going to show up." She plopped in the chair to the side of his desk, an arm's length away. "Actually he's pretty sure we scared him totally away."

"How in the world did that happen? I thought you were going to be concealed." He heard the savage ring to his words and clamped his jaws together to keep from saying anything more that he would regret.

"We were. I think the kidnapper had night-vision goggles like we did. That's about the only way he could have seen the agents in the boat hidden behind that abandoned dock. It was pitch-dark out there on the water."

"How did he escape the other boats?"

Madison lifted her shoulders in a shrug. "I don't know. You would think this guy knows something we don't. It's as if he just vanished on the lake. A figment of our imaginations."

"Could anyone see him? Make out any of his features?"

She shook her head. "He wore a black ski mask or something like that. It was hard to tell." She massaged the knot of tension forming on the side of her neck. "He may still call again."

J.T. shot her a piercing look. "Who are you kidding? Our chance is over. We— I blew it."

"I don't understand this whole situation. He waited two days to ask for a ransom. He had you leave the money in an isolated part of the lake with a lot of hiding places to conceal us. He gave us hours to get set up to wait for him. Either this man is very dumb, which I don't believe, or he is up to something else I haven't been able to figure out."

"How about to torment me further?"

"Maybe. That would fit in with someone you put away in prison."

"Yes, it does." J.T. scraped his hand over the stubble of his three-day-old beard. He knew he looked a sight, but he just didn't care. "I need to tell Kim and Neil what happened."

"I'd like to come with you."

"You should get that rest your boss ordered you to get."

"It isn't gonna happen. You should get some yourself."

"It isn't gonna happen." He shoved to his feet. "I don't want to wake them if they actually went to sleep last night. Care to walk to Emma and Colin's? I could use the fresh air. Maybe it will clean out the cobwebs in my mind."

"That might do me some good, too. Crouching in that thicket most of the night made me stiff all over. Walking should help loosen me up again."

J.T. offered her his hand. The softness of her skin against his jolted him and caused him to pull harder than he should have. Madison came up too fast and nearly knocked him back into his chair. He managed to catch himself and steady her against him. He took a deep breath. The scent of apples and cinnamon surrounded him. An interesting combination. Again he was reminded of a piece of apple pie.

The realization he continued to hold her longer than necessary stunned him momentarily. What was he doing? Quickly he separated from her, trying not to inhale too deeply. Her scent was playing havoc with his senses, making him think of picnics and warm summer days, making him forget for a heartbeat that his daughter had been abducted. "Ready?"

Madison blinked. Puzzlement creased her forehead. "Yeah."

Her slow response made him wonder if she had felt that brief connection and been just as surprised by it.

He followed her out of his office, noting the almost-deserted station.

Derek stood at the counter, near the phone, reading the newspaper. The deputy glanced at J.T. and straightened. "Sir, is there anything you want me to do?"

"I'm heading to the reverend's to see my children. I want you to forward any calls I receive to my cell phone."

"Will do."

As Madison reached out to open the front door, someone pushed it in. Elizabeth and her son entered, ready to clean the place. Surprise flickered across the older woman's face.

"You're here early. Or did you even go home last night, J.T.?" Elizabeth handed her son the container of cleaning supplies and he walked toward the back.

"I've been working, but I'm heading out right now."

"Any progress on finding Ashley?"

"We're working on it." Tension threaded his response as he placed his hand at the small of Madison's back and directed her out the door.

When J.T. stepped onto the sidewalk, rosy orange streaks fanned out across the eastern sky. The gray light of dawn muted the landscape, and the quiet of a town still asleep contrasted with what had gone on the night before.

Madison looked up and down the street. "You would never think that a kidnapping occurred here. It seems so peaceful, the perfect place."

"There's no perfect place."

"Yes, there is but not here on earth."

J.T. strode down the sidewalk that ran the length of Lakeshore Drive. "After giving myself to Christ six years ago, I didn't think anything could shake my faith. Well, I was wrong."

Madison stopped, forcing J.T. to do likewise. He turned toward her, bleakness erasing any gleam from his eyes. "Don't give up hope. This is the time to cling to Christ. He's your salvation."

J.T. expelled a long breath. "I know. But when I heard my little girl asking where I was—" he laid his hand on his chest "—it felt as though my heart shattered into hundreds of pieces." His voice broke. He swallowed several times. "The pain was unbearable. Why didn't the kidnapper come after *me?* I'm the one he's angry with. Ashley has nothing to do with it."

"As much as I wish it weren't so, the innocent often suffer. God is with her."

"It didn't sound like it on that tape." J.T. started forward again.

Madison bled for him. She reached out and placed her hand on his arm. He glanced back, agony in every line on his face. "God is with her and you."

"Six years ago when I was drinking heavily after my wife's death, I thought I couldn't go any lower. Again, I was wrong. This is rock bottom."

Drinking heavily. The words knifed through Madison. Her past held her in a haunting nightmare for a few seconds before she realized she wasn't a little girl living in Chicago, but grown and in Crystal Springs.

"Right before you came in, I almost left to find something to drink. I wanted to, but I can't. Not if I'm going to find Ashley. What if she's lost to me? I don't know if I can fight the urge…" His words came to a quivering halt.

Madison planted herself in front of him and took hold of his hands. "Don't do this to yourself. Don't try to second-guess what might happen. You're strong. You'll deal with it for Kim and Neil's sakes. You have people here who will help you."

His gaze drilled into her. "You're the first person I've told about my alcoholism. I don't like sharing that past life with anyone. Kim and Neil don't even know all that I went through."

"Don't kid yourself. Your children are sharp. They knew."

His eyebrows shot up. "Well, maybe Neil knew something was going on, but I was careful not to around them."

"Probably Kim did, too. I don't usually talk about my past, either. My father was an alcoholic, and he never kicked the habit. He drank until the day he died. His liver failed him."

"How old were you?"

"Twelve. I knew, had for years."

J.T. began to walk again, clasping Madison's hand. "You know the part about drinking that was the worst?"

"No." She didn't know if she wanted to hear the answer. The whole subject of the conversation was too painful.

"The loneliness. I lost all connections with others. I lived for the next drink. It numbed my feelings to the point that I didn't feel at all."

"You can only run so long from your emotions." She'd done her share of avoiding her feelings, especially after her father's and later her brother's death. As a teenager she had rebelled until she'd gotten herself in a situation where she'd had to decide whether she was going to follow the crowd she hung with and do drugs or say no to what they offered her. Thankfully she turned to her family's minister and found a place for herself in God's house.

"Yeah, I know you eventually hit a brick wall. When I finally started A.A., I had to face everyone in the group. That's when I sought God's guidance."

"And He was there for you through that journey."

"I wouldn't have made it without Him. These past six years I've been trying my best to make it up to my children." As J.T. passed a bench on the outskirts of the park, he gestured to it. "Want to sit? I think it's still too early to see the kids."

"That would be nice. My mind wants to keep going. My body is saying slow down."

Madison sat next to J.T., their hands no longer clasped. She missed the physical connection that had offered her some solace as their conversation plunged her into her past. Finding out that J.T. was a recovering alcoholic shook her more than she cared to admit. The day before when he had said something about his problem, she'd pushed it away successfully, not able to deal with it at that moment. She never wanted to live as she had growing up with her father and his problem. It nearly destroyed her and her family.

The rosy orange streaks faded into the blue of the sky as the sun peeked over the horizon. A male cardinal flew overhead, followed by its mate. They perched on a branch of an elm tree that shaded the bench. The scent of some honeysuckle bushes to the left sprinkled the air with their sweetness. Any other time she would appreciate the beauty around her.

A station wagon drove by, slowed down when the driver saw J.T. and her and pulled over to the side of the road. A man leaned over and said, "Anything, J.T.?"

"No, Howard."

"If I can help, please let me know."

"Will do."

As the car drove away, J.T. watched it until it turned onto a side street and disappeared from view. "That's one of Neil's baseball coaches, the one I told you about from Texas who always wears his cowboy boots."

"He's a teacher?"

"No, a lay coach. He volunteers his time with the high school team and at our church. He sells real estate around here and in Central City. That's probably where he's heading."

"You have a lot of people who care what happens."

Another car turned onto Lakeshore Drive. "Yes, and since the town is waking up, let's go. I don't want to have to answer questions and hear the pity in their voices." Instead of continuing on the sidewalk, J.T. rounded the bench. "Let's cut across the park. I know a shortcut."

"And that way hopefully you won't see anyone?"

"Right. We think alike."

Yes, they did, Madison thought, remembering back to the year before. After the initial awkwardness, they had worked well together as a team on Emma's brother's murder. In all that time she had never known that J.T. had once had an alcohol problem. Were there any other secrets he was keeping? It was the secrets that destroyed a relationship— *Whoa, where in the world had that come from?* The thought took Madison totally by surprise.

Before J.T. had a chance to ring the bell at Colin's house, Kim threw open the door and fell into his embrace. "I called the station and Derek said you were coming over here and should be here any second. That was ten minutes ago." She leaned back and stared up at him, fear in her eyes. "Where have you been?"

"I didn't want to wake you up, so we stopped at the park for a while. I'm sorry, honey, if I scared you. You should have called me on my cell."

Kim's gaze widened. "I didn't think of that. I—I'm not thinking straight."

He smoothed her hair back from her face. "Did you get any rest last night."

"No! How can I?"

"I think we should talk to the doctor about getting you something to help you sleep."

"How can I sleep when Ashley is—" Kim twisted away and stalked into the house.

J.T. sighed. "I know how she feels."

"Dad, what happened last night?" Neil came into the foyer as Madison and J.T. entered the Fitzpatricks' house.

"The kidnapper never picked up the money."

Madison noticed J.T. didn't elaborate on what went down, and she understood he was trying to protect his children as long as possible. She saw Kim hanging back by the entrance into the living room. Grace stood next to her. The aroma of coffee and ham saturated the house.

"Can you two stay for breakfast? Emma and Colin

are almost finished preparing it. Knowing my nephew, I'm sure there's plenty for everyone." Grace, with her arm around Kim, stepped into the foyer.

Before J.T. could say yes or no, Madison shut the door behind her and said, "We would love to. I haven't eaten since early in the evening yesterday. I could especially use a cup of coffee."

"Great." Grace turned back into the living room with Kim.

Neil trailed his sister and Colin's aunt. J.T. didn't move.

"You're going to have to tell them everything sooner or later, J.T."

"I wish I didn't have to. The ransom drop was botched. That's not gonna sit well with them."

"It won't take long before the whole town knows."

"And they need to hear it from me." He took a step toward the living room.

Madison's cell phone rang. She flipped it open. "Spencer here."

"Where are you?"

She heard the strain in Matthew's voice. "At the Fitzpatricks' with J.T."

"The speedboat was found."

SEVEN

Day three, 5:30 a.m.: Ashley missing fifty-nine hours

J.T. paused at the entrance into Colin's living room and peered back at Madison on her cell. She stiffened, her mouth curved into a frown.

"Where was it found?"

Her question to the person on her phone alerted J.T. He swung around and waited.

"We'll be there right away. I'm sure J.T. knows where it is." Madison snapped her cell closed.

"What was found?" He stepped toward her, not wanting anyone to hear if it was bad news.

"The speedboat." She lowered her voice. "And a burned body."

All energy siphoned from his legs. He clutched the edge of a table nearby. "Burned? Ashley?"

"No!" Madison moved close. "It was an adult."

His eyelids slid shut while he dragged in a deep breath.

"The boat was on fire when it was spotted. Paul managed to put it out, but it was scorched pretty badly. Another five or ten minutes and there would have been little left. The body was in the boat."

Tension zipped through him. "Let's go."

Madison stayed put. "You need to tell your kids something."

He glanced toward the kitchen. "What? How much?" He rolled his shoulders to ease the ache in his muscles. "You're right. Thank goodness you're here to keep me focused." All he had thought about was discovering whose boat it was and who the body in it was. A lead. They had so few real ones. But his children needed reassurances, more now than ever.

J.T. headed for the kitchen, Madison right behind him. Inside he found Neil and Kim sitting at the large table with Grace between them. Colin and his twin girls were across from Grace. Emma placed a platter of scrambled eggs and thick ham slices in the center, then took her chair.

Two empty seats beckoned. The aromas—coffee, ham, biscuits—teased him. His stomach churned with hunger, but he couldn't afford to eat. Not if this new development led to finding Ashley.

J.T. forced a half smile to his face. "That looks tempting, but Madison and I have to leave. She received a call. The speedboat that we thought we saw coming to pick up the ransom was found. Burned. How bad, I don't know."

Neil leaped to his feet. "Where? Can I come?"

J.T. shook his head.

"At Eagle's Cove," Madison said behind him.

"We need to process the scene. The fewer people involved the better it is. I'll let you know something when I know it."

"I take it the ransom wasn't picked up." Emma stood and walked to the counter.

"No, it wasn't. All that happened was this speedboat approached. The man driving must have seen something that spooked him and he made a U-turn." Madison came to J.T.'s side.

"Here, take these." Emma brought two steaming mugs of coffee to J.T. and Madison.

J.T. took a sip. "I'll call when I have news." He walked to the table and kissed Kim on the top of her head. "Things may be looking up, honey. Eat my share of breakfast."

"Can't you stay and have some before you go to Eagle's Cove?" Grace picked up the platter and spooned some eggs onto her plate. "The boat isn't going anywhere now that you have it."

Always in the back of his mind he felt the clock ticking down. The longer Ashley was gone, the harder it would be to find her. A memory of kissing Ashley goodnight the evening before she'd vanished sprang into his thoughts, producing a constriction in his chest. He began to walk toward the exit. "Not now. Thanks."

"J. T. Logan, you need to take care of yourself. You need to eat." Grace's hands rested on her waist.

"I'll grab something later. Promise." He hurried from the room before they convinced him to take the time to sit down and eat something. How could he when Ashley might be out there somewhere—hungry, thirsty, alone?

Madison caught up with him on the porch. She handed him two slices of ham sandwiched between two sections of a large biscuit. "Here. We can eat this and walk at the same time."

He bit into the buttered biscuit. "Hmm. Grace makes the best ones in town." He descended the steps and started for the sheriff's office.

When he approached his Jeep outside the office, he slipped behind the steering wheel. "Eagle's Cove is a secluded spot on the other side of the lake. It's about twenty minutes away from here."

"Do you think the person burned in the boat is the kidnapper?"

"I doubt it. If so, who set fire to the boat? Mostly likely the kidnapper, covering his tracks."

"What if he set the fire and fell before he could get away?"

"I suppose that is possible, but not likely."

Day three, 6:30 a.m.: Ashley missing sixty hours

The stench of the charred remains of the boat and body filled the cove. As J.T. descended the hill to the shore, he spied the body, burned beyond recognition, propped up in the driver's seat as though he'd steered the hull up onto the beach. The reeking odor of scorched flesh overpowered every other smell. His stomach gurgled its protest. Bile rose into his throat.

"What do we have?" J.T. stepped to one side of the craft to inspect the crime scene.

"One of our patrol boats saw the fire and investigated. Paul used an extinguisher to try and put the fire out." Matthew Hendricks gestured toward what little was left.

"As you can see, they didn't reach the scene in time. I don't know if we'll be able to get much. I guess we're lucky to have this. If Paul hadn't seen the smoke, there would be little left to process."

Madison leaned toward the victim and examined the hands. "Doesn't look like we'll be able to get any fingerprints."

"Maybe dental records will help us identify him." The lead agent removed his FBI ball cap and wiped the back of his hand across his forehead. "The medical examiner should be here shortly."

"Do we know whose boat this is?" Madison circled it, being careful not to disturb any evidence. She squatted and studied it. "J.T., do you know anyone with a boat that has a name that starts with *F-a*."

He came around to where she was. The back was black with most of it burned, except for the partial letters that looked like an *F* and an *A*.

She slanted a glance toward him. "Any boats reported missing?"

"You know now that I think about it my neighbor, Ross Morgan, has a speedboat about this size and the name of his is Fanfare." J.T. flipped open his cell and punched in a number. This could be the lead they were looking for, the kidnapper's first mistake. "Derek, has anyone reported a boat missing?"

"The Lakeshore Marina called about a half hour ago, when the man who owns the marina came to work. Ross Morgan's boat has been stolen. I was gonna head out there when Susan came in to answer the phones."

"Anyone spoken to Ross?"

"No one answered at his house."

J.T. straightened and moved toward the body in the driver's seat. He tried not to breathe too deeply as he bent over the remains to see if he could tell if it was his neighbor. "I'll handle the theft."

He closed his phone and continued his inspection. The body was about the same height as Ross, but that was about all he could tell. He stepped back, the thought making his stomach roil.

"Does this belong to Ross Morgan?"

He looked at Madison. "I believe so. It was reported stolen about a half hour ago."

"Is this him?" Madison pointed toward the body.

"I don't know, but my neighbor isn't home and usually he is at this time of day."

"Let's check it out while the crime scene is being processed."

"We're on the same page. We can stop by the marina first and see if anyone saw anything. Then we need to pay Ross a visit even if I have to go all the way to Central City to his work."

Day three, 7:30 a.m.: Ashley missing sixty-one hours

We're on the same page. Madison couldn't get those words out of her head as J.T. pulled up in front of Ross Morgan's house, just two doors down from J.T.'s. The same place where the barking dog had been poisoned two days before. Coincidence? She didn't trust coincidences.

"Let's hope this gives us more information than the marina." J.T. climbed from his Jeep and pocketed his keys.

"No wonder the boat was stolen. There's no security to speak of." Madison walked beside him up to the Morgans' house.

J.T. grinned. "Fred watches the place at night until the owner shows up in the morning."

"And Fred promptly falls asleep."

"In his defense, we don't have much crime—that is—" J.T. massaged the back of his neck. "Forget I said that. Crime has hit this little town big-time."

J.T. rang the doorbell and waited for a good minute before trying it again, pressing his finger on it for ten seconds. He frowned, his eyebrows knitting together.

"Didn't Derek say earlier he couldn't get anyone on the phone? Obviously Ross and Jill have gone to work."

J.T. shot her a skeptical look. "Before seven in the morning? That's a bit early for them to go to work. What if something happened to them?"

While he opened the screen door and pounded on the wooden one, she peered into the large, living room window. "Everything looks like it's in place. No signs of a struggle or anything. Maybe we should check out the garage. See if a car is in there."

After another minute J.T. backed away, letting the screen slam closed. A perplexed expression narrowed his gaze, glued to the entrance. "How do you feel about taking a ride to—"

The door swung open. Ross stood there, his hair messy, his eyes sleepy. He was barefoot in a pair of jeans and a white T-shirt. "J.T.? What are you doing here? What time is it? Six?"

"Seven-thirty, and we've been trying to get you for

over an hour. Derek Nelson called you several times. You've been here the whole time?"

Ross nodded slowly, pushing his fingers through his unruly hair. "Yes, I've been here all night. I guess I didn't hear the phone." He rubbed his forehead, then his eyes. "I never sleep hard. I don't understand why I didn't hear the phone ringing."

The last sentence was almost spoken as though she and J.T. weren't on his front porch. Ross pivoted and left the foyer. J.T. entered, watching the man retreat into his living room. Madison came up beside J.T.

"What's going on?"

J.T. leaned in so he could see into the room. "He's checking his phone messages."

A minute later Ross returned. "I thought maybe Jill might have called."

"She isn't here with you?" J.T. scanned the hallway that led to the back of the house.

"No." The man's face reddened, and he lowered his gaze.

"Where is she?"

"She's visiting—her mother." Ross reestablished eye contact. "There was an emergency and she had to go see her mother for a few days. I was just checking to make sure she made it all right. It's about ten hours by car so she must still be driving. She had to leave in the middle of the night."

As the man rambled on, giving them more information than they needed, Madison could tell he was lying. He had crossed his arms and his gaze kept sliding away. She would definitely be checking into Ross Morgan, in depth.

"Why was Deputy Nelson trying to call me?" Ross finally asked, uncrossing his arms and letting them fall limply to his sides.

"Your speedboat was stolen last night. We found it this morning on fire with someone still sitting in the driver's seat, charred beyond recognition."

Ross's jaw dropped. "My boat! There was a burned body in it?"

"Yes. What remains of it is beached at Eagle's Cove."

"Why would anyone want my boat? There were a lot nicer ones at the marina. How in the world did it catch on fire? Who is the dead man?"

"Good questions. If one of the patrols hadn't seen the smoke, the boat would have been burned so badly, that we wouldn't have known it was yours." Madison walked a few paces toward the living room, her gaze sweeping the room for any sign of something not quite right.

"We don't know who the man is. The boat was involved in the ransom drop for Ashley." The tight edge to J.T.'s voice conveyed the fragile control he had on himself.

Madison peered over her shoulder at him, seeing his mouth pinched into a tight line. She wanted to lessen his pain.

The color drained from Ross's face. "J.T., I'm so sorry. I didn't even know there had been a ransom demand. What happened?"

"It was botched."

Ross's shoulders sagged. He swiped his hand across his forehead. "I can't believe the kidnapper used my boat." He paused, tilted his head. "So the dead body is the kidnapper?"

"I don't think so, but if it is, we still don't know where Ashley is."

Suppressed emotions laced J.T.'s voice. Madison wound her way back to J.T.'s side. She wanted to take his hand and hold it for moral support, but she didn't. Frustration gripped her. It was becoming more difficult to keep a professional distance.

Ross straightened. "If I can help in any way, please let me know." He strode toward the front door and grasped its handle, ushering them toward it.

Time to leave. Something wasn't right here. J.T.'s neighbor was hiding something. What? And was it connected to Ashley's kidnapping?

J.T. and Madison thanked Ross for his time and left.

J.T. stopped halfway down the sidewalk and surveyed the neighborhood. "He's lying."

"I think so, too. I'll start checking him out when we get back to the station."

An elderly lady in a flowery dress came out of the house next to the Morgans' and shuffled down the driveway to get her newspaper. J.T.'s grim expression melted some as his gaze lit upon the woman. She saw him and waved.

He made a beeline for her. "Marge knows everything that goes on around here." He nodded toward Marge. "How are you doing?"

"My hip is giving me some problems, but that's for another day. The more important question is, how are you doing?"

"Not good until I get my little girl back."

"I'm praying every day and night for her return."

"As the whole church is, and I appreciate those prayers." J.T. turned toward Madison. "Have you met FBI agent Madison Spencer?"

Madison smiled at the older woman. "I interviewed you the other day. You were most helpful. She told me about a car that she had seen on the street the day before, parked a few doors down from your house."

J.T. tensed and started to say something.

"But it turned out," Madison hurried on, "to be a teenager named Kyle waiting for his girlfriend to get home."

"Kyle and Neil are friends. His mother and his older brother clean the station." J.T.'s anxiety seeped from him. "Marge, can you think of anything else strange that has occurred in the past few days? Sometimes small things turn out to be big leads."

The older lady scrunched up her mouth and tapped her finger against her chin. "I see you were coming from Ross and Jill's. You know, she left him early yesterday evening."

"She did?" J.T. shifted his attention back to the Morgans' house, his gaze narrowed.

"They had a big fight. I was out in my backyard watering my roses when I heard them shouting. I think she poisoned their dog." Marge leaned close to J.T. "You know she hated that dog. Once she told Ross all his pet was good for was yelping and driving her crazy."

J.T. picked up Marge's newspaper and handed it to her. "If you think of anything else, please let me know."

"I'll think on it. I want Ashley back."

He touched her arm. "Me, too."

After the older woman went back into her house,

Madison walked with J.T. to his Jeep. She opened the passenger door and climbed in. "Why did Ross lie about when Jill left? Do you think she is capable of poisoning their dog?"

When J.T. situated himself behind the wheel, he twisted toward her. "I don't have an answer to those questions, but then the Morgans have only lived here for a year. Jill never seemed the type to poison a dog. She was always nice to my kids." J.T.'s mouth tightened in a scowl.

"Did she go out of her way to be friendly?"

J.T. gripped the steering wheel. "I don't think so, but truthfully I never thought about it. People in Crystal Springs *are* friendly. I never questioned the motives behind that friendliness."

"I know you think it's someone from your past, but we can't rule out other possibilities."

"Like it might be someone from Crystal Springs?"

"Yes."

"I don't want to ignore anything. The Morgans are definitely worth checking out and keeping an eye on. Ross is hiding something."

"Some people are very good at erecting a false facade. With that in mind, I would like to start looking into people who moved to Crystal Springs in the past year, especially people connected to you in any way."

"For the record I still think it's someone from my past in Chicago." J.T. turned the key and the engine roared to life. "But you're right. Everyone is a suspect until proven otherwise." He pulled away from the curb and glanced toward her. "But I feel instead of ruling people out, we are just adding more and more to the list of suspects."

"I'll do it quietly and utilize Paul so no one in your office will know."

"That's probably best. I have to live with these people when you leave."

Day four, 7:30 p.m.: Ashley missing seventy-three hours

At an evening prayer service for Ashley, Madison sat sandwiched between Emma and J.T. Kim and Neil were on his other side. Madison peered around her—not one seat was empty. People even stood in the back and along the side aisles.

Colin rose to offer one last prayer. Madison bowed her head, her gaze gliding down the row. The haggard lines in J.T.'s face had deepened over the course of each day. She wanted to take him into her arms and hold him until his daughter was found alive.

The main reason J.T. had stopped long enough to come to the prayer vigil for Ashley was because Kim had asked. She wasn't doing well, either. Her eyes held a bruised expression and even her hair was unkempt. Kim's growing silence worried Madison.

"Lord, we ask You to bring Ashley home and to protect her. Please keep her safe and in Your hands. Be with J.T. and his family in their time of need. Touch them with Your bountiful love and mercy. In the name of Jesus Christ, our Savior. Amen."

Madison had always liked how Colin communicated with God: simple and to the point. The power of hundreds of prayers gave her an added boost of energy. She had only begun her search into the background of the people who had recently moved to the town. So far she had discovered Jill Morgan had indeed left her husband the day before in the late afternoon, not evening and the vet had been suspicious the last time their dog had been brought in for an injury. But if Jill had poisoned her dog, then why did she report it to the police unless she did it to keep Ross from finding out the truth? And why had Ross lied about when Jill had left? What else had they been lying about? So many questions and not nearly enough answers.

Madison rose as J.T. did. He'd waited until most of the people had filed out of the church.

"Daddy, do you think the prayers helped?"

That was the first full sentence Kim had spoken since J.T. and she had picked up the children to come to the prayer vigil.

J.T. wound his arm around his daughter's shoulders. "Definitely. That's one thing you can do to help your sister."

"Then I'll keep them up. I just didn't know if they were helping."

"Always. We have to practice patience. God works in His time, not ours." He hugged her against his side.

"Are we going home tonight?" Neil sidestepped toward the center aisle.

Kim followed her brother from the pew. "Yeah, can we?"

"Yes."

"Now?" An eager gleam pushed the dull flatness from Kim's eyes for a few seconds.

"I've got some things to wrap up down at the station, then we can go home."

Neil saw a friend and headed toward him while Kim continued to cling to J.T. Short of prying her loose, he wasn't going to get away easily.

At the back of the sanctuary he stopped in front of Colin. "Thank you for putting this together. I should be by to pick Neil and Kim up in a couple of hours."

"We'll take care of them until you can. Don't worry."

Madison hung back while J.T. talked with Colin. She studied the people left in the church. Living most of her life in a big city, she missed the feeling of family in a small town. No wonder J.T. had come home to Crystal Springs. She hoped no one from here was involved in the kidnapping. She didn't like the fact that Ross Morgan had a sealed juvenile record. What was the man hiding? Even though he wasn't really from Crystal Springs, he was J.T.'s neighbor.

"Ready to leave?" J.T. approached her.

She glimpsed Emma taking Neil and Kim into the foyer. "Go with your children. I can take care of the few loose ends. If anything breaks, I'll call."

"We should be getting the medical examiner's report soon on the body in the boat. I want to be there for that."

She stopped him moving toward the double wooden doors. "You need some sleep."

He peered back at her, his gaze slipping to her hand on his arm. "And you don't?"

"Yes, and I plan to get some or I won't be able to put two words together to form a coherent sentence."

"I'll only stay a few hours. Besides, who would take you to the station?"

She grinned, releasing her hold on him. "You, on your way to pick up your kids at the Fitzpatricks'. I can call you about the medical examiner's report."

He turned toward her. "I want to know who that man was."

"We may never know who he was."

He sucked in a deep breath. "I know. Why can't it be easy? The man was the kidnapper, or his best friend. I hope we'll discover who he was, raid his home and find Ashley alive and well."

"We'll get a break." She walked beside J.T. as they left the church.

At his Jeep she scanned the parking lot. Cars streamed out of it. She noticed that Emma, Grace and Colin had already taken Kim and Neil to their house. For a moment the sensation that someone was watching crawled up her spine, leaving a chilled film of perspiration in its wake.

Inside the confines of the car Madison tried to relax her taut muscles, but she couldn't shake the feeling.

J.T.'s gaze riveted to hers. "You feel it, too."

She nodded.

He made a slow sweep of the area, his eyes narrowed as though that would help him see into the dark shadows. "He's out there somewhere close. I can feel him."

"This does seem personal."

His grip on the steering showed white knuckles. "It's a criminal I've put in jail who wants revenge. I'd call that pretty personal."

"What if it isn't? I've discovered Ross Morgan isn't

the upstanding citizen he's led everyone to believe. What other secrets are there in Crystal Springs?"

J.T. opened his mouth to say something when his cell phone rang. He answered it. His frown deepened as he listened. When he ended the call, a storm brewed in the depths of his eyes. "That was Kirk. No positive identification on our burned corpse. He was dead before he was set on fire. There wasn't any smoke in his lungs. He was shot, up close and personal."

"How about the bullet?"

"Too damaged to get ballistics on it."

"So there's nothing we can use?"

"Not exactly. Central City police did phone to say there was a missing person report filed this evening. He's a short-order cook at a grill on this side of the city. He's about the size of the man in the boat."

"Who is it? Can we confirm it with dental records?"

"Max Dillard, and the police are checking about dental records, but they aren't too hopeful."

Madison sat forward, angling around to face J.T. "The name isn't familiar?"

"No, but they're going to fax a picture if they can find a photo of the man or have an artist draw one from his coworkers' description. He's been working at the grill for about a year." J.T. started his Jeep and backed out of the parking space.

"Maybe he's moved on and is not really missing."

"The owner insisted something was wrong. Max was all excited about a chance to earn some extra money. He was sweet on a waitress at the grill and had a date with her tonight after their shift. He never showed up for work today."

Could this be the break they were looking for? *Father, please let it be.*

When J.T. pulled up in front of the station, he switched off the Jeep and started to get out.

"Where are you going?"

He glanced over his shoulder, then pivoted around to face her. "Inside."

"So you can sit by the fax machine and wait for a picture that might not come for hours or until tomorrow. We have pictures of each of the felons on your list. We can compare them. Go home. Your children need to see you. You need to see your children. Be the parent, J.T."

He scowled. "I am. I'm being Ashley's father."

"How about Kim and Neil's?"

He flinched. "That's low. They aren't in trouble. Ashley is."

She needed to shake some common sense into him and make him slow down before he collapsed. "In case you haven't noticed, both of your other children are in trouble, especially Kim. They may be trying to hide their pain from you, but it's there for anyone to see if you stand still long enough to look."

He blew out a frustrated breath. "You certainly know how to make a guy feel bad."

She took his hand nearest her, trying to ignore the quickening of her heartbeat at the touch of his skin against hers. "For the next twelve hours be the parent. Forget you're the sheriff. Let us do our job. We're good at it. I promise if there's anything important I'll call you immediately even if it's in the wee hours of the morning."

"You aren't going to your motel to get some sleep?"

"Not if it will keep you at home. I'll catch some shut-eye in the back room. That cot of yours isn't too bad." She smiled. "Is it a deal? I'll hold down the fort while you get some rest. Will you trust me to see to everything?"

He turned his hand within hers and grasped it. The connection sent her heart beating even faster. The intensity in his eyes nearly unraveled her composure.

"I do trust you."

Those words made her soar. Trust didn't come lightly for J.T. and for him to say that meant a lot.

"You'll call even if you aren't sure it's important."

"Nope."

He blinked.

"The idea is for you to get some rest so you can function tomorrow. You will have to trust my judgment on what is important and what isn't. Can you?"

He looked long and hard at her. Seconds ticked into a full minute. Normally his expression would be closed to an observer, but because of his exhaustion, she saw the war of emotions flitting across his features. Finally resignation won.

"Okay. I'll be back at the station first thing tomorrow morning."

Madison checked the clock on the dashboard. "Not before eight. Twelve hours."

He gave her a nod, released her hand and grasped the steering wheel. For an irrational moment she longed to touch the taut arm near her and massage the tension from it. She averted her head, closed her eyes, inhaling deeply the air laced with his fresh, woodsy scent and fumbled for the handle.

"See you tomorrow morning." She hurried toward the station, aware that J.T. hadn't left yet.

Inside, she heard his vehicle's engine roar to life and leaned back against the closed door. What was happening to her? She never had trouble keeping her professional life separate. J.T. was changing all that, but even after Ashley came home and the case was resolved, there were too many reasons why a relationship with J.T. would never work.

EIGHT

Day four, 5:30 a.m.: Ashley missing eighty-three hours

J.T. cradled his first cup of coffee for the new day, sure it wouldn't be his last. The evening before exhaustion finally took over and sleep came—for a few hours. Then the dreams—no, nightmares—invaded. A parade of criminals assailed him with all the reasons why they were the ones who kidnapped Ashley, their sinister faces seared into his mind as though they branded him.

"Dad, did you get any rest?" Neil trudged into the kitchen, went directly to the pot of coffee and poured himself a mug.

"Some. How about you?"

Neil took the chair next to J.T. at the glass table, rested his elbows on the plaid place mat and sipped his drink. "Some. I heard you get up and decided that I wasn't fooling anyone. Four hours of sleep was about all I'm going to get. I can't get Ashley out of my mind. I remember the last time I saw her when I dropped her off at school." His son set the mug on the mat and stared at the black liquid as though he could picture Ashley's face in it. "I didn't even wave goodbye like I usually do because I was running late. She did. I saw her in the rear-view mirror as I pulled away from the curb."

Neil's last words, uttered in a hoarse whisper, sliced through J.T. as if he had been shot. He, too, remembered times he should have slowed down and spent more time with Ashley—with all his children. "She knows you love her." He said that as much to reassure himself as Neil.

His son's gaze riveted to his. "How do we become so busy that we don't see the little things that are so important? Like my sister waving goodbye to me?"

J.T. put down his own cup, his hands encircling it. The warm ceramic felt nice against his cold fingers. "Good question. I need to be here for you and Kim, but I also need to be the sheriff and find Ashley. It's hard to be everything at once."

Neil picked up his mug and took a long sip. "Don't worry about me, Dad. I know Ashley must come first."

When had his son grown up? Looking at him, J.T. saw a mature young man who would be leaving in a few months. Neil would be moving out of his home and going to college. His son would be beginning a new phase of his life. Mixed feelings—happiness, sadness— bombarded J.T. "Kim is taking this hard."

"I know. She thinks she's responsible for Ashley's kidnapping."

J.T.'s grip on his cup strengthened, strain flowing down his arms all the way to his fingertips. "She isn't. This doesn't have anything to do with you or her at all. It's me. I'm the reason."

"What are we going to do if we can't find—"

J.T. heard footsteps coming down the hallway and placed his finger to his mouth. Neil glanced toward the doorway at the same time Kim came into the room.

His son smiled at his younger sister. "It's about time you got up. Dad and I have been up for—" he shifted his gaze to the clock on the wall "—at least a half hour. But I guess a girl has got to get her beauty sleep."

Kim yawned and plowed her fingers through the mass of curls about her face. She peered out the window. "It's still dark."

"Not for long." J.T. shoved himself to his feet and crossed the room to Kim. He took her into his arms and held her for a long moment. "I'm cooking breakfast. How do you feel about pancakes?"

She shrugged away and folded her arms over her chest, a dull look on her face. "I'm not hungry." She shuffled toward the table and plopped in the chair at the end, slouching forward.

"Honey, you need to eat something. It isn't every day I volunteer to cook your favorite breakfast." J.T. settled his hand on her shoulder.

She yanked away. "I bet Ashley isn't eating, so I shouldn't. That's the least I can do since—" Swallowing hard, Kim swung around to stare out the window, stiff as if she were frozen in place.

J.T. drew in a deep, composing breath, his own nerves stretched to the limit. The windowpane reflected her mutinous expression. He grasped the back of the chair and scooted it around so she faced him. He clasped both of her upper arms and knelt in front of her.

At first his daughter refused to look at him. He waited with the fragile patience he mustered to get through to Kim. Finally her gaze connected with his. The pain he glimpsed in her eyes mirrored his own. He wasn't going to let the kidnapper harm Kim, too—even emotionally.

"You are *not* to blame. You did *not* take Ashley. You did *not* want anything to happen to her."

A tear coursed down her cheek. "But, Daddy, I told you I wished I didn't have a sister. I got my wish. I caused this to happen."

He inhaled a shallow breath, but it wasn't enough to fill his lungs. They burned from the lack of rich oxygen. "You didn't," he managed to whisper after another deep gulp of air. "You had nothing to do with this. It's not unusual for siblings to wish that."

"Yeah, shrimp. I did several times when you bugged me too much. Remember that time you followed me and Kyle to the park and wouldn't leave me alone?" Neil got up and walked over to the counter to refill his coffee.

"But you two were meeting girls."

"Exactly my point."

"Honey, you didn't wish this to happen to Ashley."

Kim's tears continued to fall. "God must hate me. I shouldn't have thought that."

"God loves you and forgives you. Why can't you forgive yourself?" J.T. massaged his hands up and down her arms, her skin so cold. He wanted to transmit some warmth into his daughter, but he was afraid he had none to give.

Kim hiccuped. "I'm a bad person. I—" Another hiccup sounded in the quiet.

J.T. hauled her against him, holding her so fiercely that Kim finally had to murmur, "Daddy, I can't breathe."

He pulled away a few inches and looked down at her. "Sorry, honey." He hitched up his mouth at one corner. "I want you to realize how important you and your brother are to me. You are not the bad person."

"The one who is bad—no, evil—is the kidnapper, shrimp." Neil passed Kim and tousled her hair. "And I don't want you to forget that. We'll get him, though, won't we, Dad?"

J.T. nodded, praying it was the truth.

The doorbell chimed. Its sound knifed through the silence and separated J.T. and Kim.

He headed toward the front of the house. "Kim, get out the ingredients for pancakes. We're having a big breakfast, you two." He opened the door to find Madison standing before him.

Behind her, dawn crept through the yard, lightening the darkness to a muted gray. She smiled and the gesture went straight through him, warming some of the coldness.

"I saw your lights on." Madison walked into the house. "Your dark circles aren't as pronounced as yesterday. You must have gotten some sleep."

"A few hours. How about you?"

"About the same."

He grinned slightly. "We're quite a pair." He shut the door, wishing he could shut the real world out that easily. "What have you heard?"

"The burned corpse was finally identify as Max Dillard. The police got the dental records because he was in the army. He isn't one of the criminals you put away."

He gestured toward the manila folder she carried. "Do you have his photo?"

"Yes." She handed it to him.

He flipped it open and immediately realized it wasn't anyone he'd ever seen. He rarely forgot a face, especially of someone he arrested. He'd been staring at their photos for days. He saw them in his sleep. "So now, we go interview the girlfriend. Maybe she'll remember something that will help us."

"Sounds like a plan. I have her address in Central City."

"I guess she wouldn't appreciate us waking her up. I'm fixing breakfast for the kids. Join us, then we can head to Central City." The invitation sounded so normal. When would his life ever return to some kind of normalcy?

Madison followed him into the kitchen and greeted his children while he took out the griddle and gathered the ingredients on the counter to mix into batter. He listened to Madison make small talk with Neil and Kim and realized she fit right in with his family. Even last year when they had been on the murder case together, she had gotten along well with his children.

J.T. stirred the batter until the lumps were gone. Did she want a family? The question popped into his mind when he heard her elicit a laugh from Kim. It stunned him. When had he begun to look at her in a different light?

"Yep, Daddy managed to burn the pancakes the first time he fixed them." Kim chuckled again.

"And we're letting him prepare them now?" Madison waved her hand at him. "Isn't there something wrong with this picture?"

J.T. spun around with a metal spatula in his hand,

brandishing it like a weapon. "Anytime any of you wants to help me, go right ahead. I won't stand in your way."

"Oh, no, Dad. We'll let you do all the work. You need the practice." Neil lounged back in the chair as though nothing was going to budge him.

J.T. pointed at each one of them, as relaxed as if they didn't have a care in the world. Madison stretched out her legs and crossed them at her ankles. Kim hooked her arm on the back of her chair. He wished he could preserve this moment, but reality was only a heartbeat away. "I think there's something wrong with *this* picture."

"Daddy—" Kim nodded toward the griddle behind him "—the pancakes are burning."

He whirled around and quickly removed the six, slightly charred pancakes. After putting the next batch on to cook, he brought the platter to the table. "There's more where that came from."

Neil scooted close to the table and forked several. "That's what we're afraid of, but I'm starved so I'll make the sacrifice and eat these."

Kim leaned close to Madison and whispered loudly so everyone could hear, "He'll eat anything. He's a human garbage disposal."

"I am not, shrimp." Neil stabbed the air with his fork, his first mouthful of pancakes on its end.

"Hey, you're supposed to wait for grace." Kim exaggerated a pout.

"Tell you what, Kim and Neil, I'll say it. Then he can eat them while they are still warm." Madison straightened in the chair.

"You mean burned."

J.T. moved toward the table with the metal spatula still in hand. Listening to Kim tease Neil gladdened J.T.'s heart. Somehow they would find Ashley and he would put his family back together. Madison made it seem possible. "That sounds like a good idea." J.T. bowed his head.

Madison linked hands with J.T. and Kim. "Father, bless this food and each one in this room. Please bring Ashley home to us and watch out for her in the meantime. Give us the strength to do what's right. In Jesus Christ's name. Amen."

The prayer sobered the moment and brought the real world crashing down upon J.T. He finished preparing the pancakes then sat at the table, the easy camaraderie gone. Guilt nibbled at him. Scanning the faces around the table, he came to the conclusion the others felt the same guilt he did. For a few minutes they had enjoyed themselves while Ashley was out there somewhere.

J.T. stared down at his three pancakes and couldn't muster the will to eat. His stomach coiled into a huge knot. He picked at his food.

After lavishing butter and syrup on her stack, Madison brought the first bite to her mouth and chewed. "These are good." She locked gazes with each one of them at the table. "You all haven't done anything wrong. Eat."

J.T. didn't want his children to feel guilty for enjoying anything, even a little time away from the case. "Yeah, Madison's right. You need to eat." He took a bite of his pancakes and, although they tasted bland to him, he made a point of chewing and swallowing them.

Day four, 8:30 a.m.: Ashley missing eighty-six hours

The outskirts of Central City loomed in front of Madison. She slid a glance toward J.T. Since they'd left his house over a half hour ago, he'd been silent as he'd driven, the strong line of his jaw transmitting his stress. As expected, he was living and breathing this case 24-7. She wasn't sure how he kept himself together. Sheer willpower and determination.

She angled toward him. "I think you've got some hidden talents you haven't told anyone about."

He arched an eyebrow. "I do?"

"Breakfast was good."

"You didn't have Neil's pancakes."

"True, but when you kept your attention on them, they were fine. I never took the time to really learn to cook. I know I should, but work has always filled so much of my life that it was easier to order in or eat out."

He gave her a half grin. "For me, I either had to learn or I would have had a rebellion on my hands. My children like to eat and I refuse to order pizza every other night."

"Survival. That's a good reason."

"What are you going to do when you get married?"

Madison mimicked him quirking his eyebrow. "I do believe that is a sexist comment, Mr. Logan."

He chuckled. "You're probably right."

She liked hearing his laugh even if it was brief. "Besides, I'm married to my job. You know the kind of hours we keep."

"So no one is waiting for you in Chicago?"

"Not that I know of. I was engaged once and that is the closest I want to come to getting married." As she stated what she had believed for three years, the usual conviction wasn't there. She couldn't get out of her mind the few minutes of camaraderie at the table in J.T.'s kitchen this morning. She'd felt a part of his family and liked that a lot.

He turned onto a side street from the main highway. "What happened? Why didn't you get married?"

"My fiancé decided my job wasn't something he could handle. Of course, he didn't let me know that. He just decided not to show up at the church the day of the wedding. He had his best man deliver my Dear Jane letter to the bride's room where I was getting dressed in my gown."

"I'm sorry. It sounds like he was a coward."

"Among other things. I know I was lucky to find out before the wedding what kind of man he really was, but it hurt badly nevertheless. I didn't see it coming. It makes me doubt my ability to read people, which isn't good for my job."

"So he's the reason you don't want to get married? He's only one guy."

"But he's right. My job is demanding and dangerous. You know that better than most. If I hadn't been so busy, I would have seen it coming."

He pulled up in front of the diner where Max had worked. "I know what a job can do to a relationship. My wife told me when we got married that she could handle the danger part of my job as long as I didn't shut her out. It didn't work."

"When did you start shutting your wife out?"

"When she became pregnant with Ashley, I think. I figured out that my talking shop upset her more than she ever let on. She'd become quite good at covering up her fear."

"Were you drinking?"

"I drank occasionally. I started drinking seriously shortly before Ashley was born."

Madison put her hand on the handle. "So telling your wife had been good therapy and the bottle became your outlet after that."

"You can't keep things inside of you for long. Something has to give." J.T. exited the Jeep and caught her gaze over its top. "In my case my life."

She peered at the diner with its large picture window with the name of the place plastered in bold red letters across the top of the glass—Big Mama's Diner. "How do you want to do this?"

"Let's play it by ear. I don't imagine Max's girlfriend has anything to hide. She did call the police about the fact that Max was missing."

"Good cop, good cop. I like that."

Madison entered the oblong eatery with the traditional counter, red leather stools and red leather booths. The decor was almost nonexistent—off-white walls with a few old posters of Central City. She headed toward an empty booth at the end by the restrooms and pay phone and slid in. J.T. sat across from her.

A waitress with Nancy embroidered across the top right corner of her white shirt stopped at the booth. She removed the pencil stuck in her curly hair. "What can I get you two?"

"Is Paula working today?" Madison took her FBI badge out of her purse and showed it to the woman.

Nancy's eyes grew round. "This is about Max, isn't it?"

"Yes, do you know anything about why he would be on Crystal Lake driving a speedboat?" J.T. handed back the menus to the waitress.

"No, and for the record I didn't like the man. I warned Paula about him. Shifty eyes if you ask me. He came here this time last year, bragging about how great a cook he was, how he had worked years at a cafe in Southern Illinois and people used to come for miles around to eat his food." Her mouth pinched and brows lowered into a frown, Nancy scanned the half-filled diner. "He ain't done anything like that here. This is about as crowded as it gets. I'll get Paula. She's in back." The waitress started to turn away but stopped. "Sure you don't want anything?"

"I'll take a cup of coffee." Madison looked toward the back behind the counter but only saw an older woman whom she doubted was Max's girlfriend.

"Me, too."

While Nancy went to get the coffee and Paula, Madison shook her head, chuckling. "Where do people get that shifty eyes means a person is a criminal?"

"Beats me. But in Max's case what was he doing in Crystal Springs? Was he in on the kidnapping and had a falling-out with his partner?"

"Yeah, those shifty eyes are a dead giveaway."

"At least they weren't beady ones."

Madison laughed. "Quit it. I won't be able to keep a straight face when we interview Paula."

"Shh. I think she's coming over here."

Madison glanced over her shoulder and saw a young woman in her late twenties with stringy brown hair that hung limply to her shoulders making her way toward them with two cups of coffee.

"Nancy said you wanted to see me. You're with the police. I've already talked with two yesterday afternoon. Don't you all share your information?" Wariness lined Max's girlfriend's face, her tone surly. She plopped the mugs down in front of them, some of Madison's coffee sloshing out.

"I'm with the FBI and we're working a kidnapping case in Crystal Springs. We needed to ask you some—"

"I don't know nothing about no kidnapping." Paula took a step back.

"I wanted to ask you about Max Dillard," Madison said quickly before the woman fled. "You reported him missing."

Surprise replaced the wary look in Paula's eyes. "Max wouldn't do no kidnapping."

"We aren't saying that he did. We just need to know about the job Max took to earn some extra money." J.T. lifted the mug to his mouth, his gaze intent on Paula.

"I don't know nothing."

"You don't know who hired him, what he was supposed to do?" Madison took her napkin and wiped up the coffee around her cup. "Someone killed him. We think the person who hired him did it. We can't find his killer without your help."

Max's girlfriend stared off into space for a long moment before returning her attention to them. "He didn't say, but I got the feeling he knew the person. We was to go out to that fancy Italian restaurant on Second Avenue. You don't get out of that place for less than a hundred dollars."

J.T. leaned forward. "Do you know how he knew the person? Male? Female?"

Paula flipped her hair behind her shoulders. "Nope. I got the impression he wasn't to talk about the job. He usually told me everything." Tears glinted in her eyes. "We'd been dating two months."

Madison withdrew a card. "If you remember anything that might help us, please give me a call."

The waitress glanced at their coffees. "Do you want a refill or anything else?"

"No, thanks." J.T. took another sip.

When Paula strode away, Madison cradled her mug and lifted it toward her mouth. "Do you believe her?"

"Yes. We still don't know if Max was an accomplice or not."

"I'm not sure it makes much difference at this point. We should go on the assumption that the person who hired Max crossed his path sometime in the past."

"Which means we need to check this guy out thoroughly. I've got Rachel working on him. I'll make sure she does an in-depth background check. We need to know his favorite color and who his third grade teacher was."

Madison started to say something when J.T.'s cell phone rang. He took the call, hope entering his expression as he listened. "We'll be there in fifteen." When he hung up, he said, "That was Central City Police. They picked up a teen who was caught stealing a car last night. His prints match the ones in the metallic blue car found in the field. They are holding him at the main station downtown."

"Let's go." Madison slipped from the booth.

After tossing a few dollars on the table to cover the coffees, J.T. walked beside her out of the café. Fifteen minutes later, he pulled into a space in the parking lot at the side of the police station. Inside one of the detectives showed J.T. and Madison to the interrogation room where they were holding the teen.

The watcher paced the length of the room, glancing toward the door that led to the basement where she was. "I've got to get rid of her. I've got to kill her. Finish what I started."

Day four, 12:30 p.m.: Ashley missing ninety hours

Madison walked into the sheriff's station next to J.T. Matthew stood before the time line up on the dry erase board, discussing something with Paul. Rachel sat at her computer, typing. Behind the front counter Derek nodded to her. A phone rang and Susan picked it up. The scent of coffee permeated the large room, a hushed level of noise.

Kirk came from the back area. "Was the trip productive?"

J.T. grinned. "Yes. There's a chance Max knew the person who hired him, and we talked with the guy who was in the metallic blue car."

"And?"

Madison noticed Matthew flip open his cell phone. "The kid is only eighteen, and when he heard about the kidnapping and his possible part in it, he was very cooperative. He saw a white car on the gravel road about the time the kidnapper would have been parked there. He said about six."

"What make, year?" Kirk asked.

"He didn't know. He glimpsed the car and hightailed it out of there. But at least we know we are looking for a white car." J.T. looked toward the head FBI agent and frowned.

"Do you know how many white cars there are?" Kirk turned around to see what J.T. was staring at.

Madison peered, too, transfixed by the excitement in Matthew's expression as he spoke to Paul.

J.T. moved toward the FBI agent. "I know it's a long shot. But it's better than nothing which is what we had when we went to Central City this morning."

"Did he know if it was a white car with an Illinois license plate?" Kirk asked from across the room.

Everyone stared at the deputy then J.T., who was approaching Matthew. Madison hurried toward the lead agent.

J.T. glanced back over his shoulder. "No, he didn't know." Then he faced Matthew. "What's happening?"

The agent smiled. "Eric Carlton was picked up crossing the state line."

NINE

Madison glanced up from studying her notes. With his arms folded over his chest and an unreadable expression on his face, J.T. stood back from the table where Eric sat in the lone interview room at the station.

"You want us to believe you won a trip to Atlantic City out of the blue and you can't remember entering any contests?" Madison shook her head slowly.

Eric looked right into her eyes. "Yes, because it's true. A five-day trip and it was awesome." He swiveled in his chair and stared at J.T. "I couldn't have kidnapped your daughter. I wasn't here. You can check."

J.T. unfolded his arms and moved toward the table, still not one bit of emotion showing. "We are. If your story checks out and there are witnesses to prove you were there, then you will be free to go. What I want to know right now is how you were informed about this trip?"

"I received it in the mail. At first I didn't believe it, but then I called the hotel and they confirmed it. The catch was I had to be there the next day if I wanted the free hotel and meals."

"And you didn't think something was odd about that?" Madison rose, needing to stretch her legs after sitting for the past hour drilling Eric on his story.

"Lady, I've learned not to look a gift horse in the mouth. I like to gamble. This was my dream vacation."

"Why didn't you tell anyone you were going to be gone?" J.T. lounged back in his chair as though he had not a care in the world.

"Who would I tell? No one will have anything to do with me since I got out of prison last year. I have an Internet business that barely makes me a living because I couldn't find a job here in town."

J.T. leaned forward. "Then why have you stayed?"

"It's my home. A Carlton has lived in that cabin for several generations."

"Let's go over this one more time." J.T. planted his arms on the table, his hands fisted. "What was the postmark—"

A rap on the door interrupted his question. Madison crossed the small room and slipped out into the hall.

"He's telling the truth." Paul gave her his notes on the calls he made to Atlantic City.

"Who paid for the trip?"

"Someone used cash."

"Did anyone at the hotel remember the person?"

Paul frowned. "Not so far. A couple of our agents in New Jersey are still checking."

"Okay, thanks. I'll tell J.T." Madison reentered the interview room, wishing she had better news.

"So you don't remember anything about the letter or the envelope?" J.T. glanced up at her, his gaze lingering for a few extra seconds.

"Nope. I threw it away in Atlantic City after I arrived."

"Where?" Madison sat again at the table across from J.T.

"Some trash can in the lobby."

Dead end. She knew it would be because too much time had passed, but she had to ask. "You're free to go. We may have more questions for you later so please don't leave town."

Eric shoved his chair back and leaped to his feet. He hurried out of the room.

Silence reigned for a good minute as J.T. stared at Madison.

Finally J.T. said, "His story checked out. I figured it would. If he had taken Ashley, he wouldn't have come back."

"But we had to talk to him. We still have the Atlantic City lead. Maybe someone at the hotel will remember the person who purchased Eric's stay."

"Cash?"

Madison nodded.

J.T. dropped his head forward, raking his hands down his face. "Why can't this be easy for once?"

Ashley sniffed the air, sensing something different in it. She cocked her head and leaned close to the doggy door, trying to figure out what it was she smelled. Then she remembered what happened the last time she hadn't eaten real fast. She'd fallen in the dark and hurt herself because the bad man didn't give her much time to eat.

Quickly she stuffed the rest of her peanut butter and jelly sandwich into her mouth, then gulped down the funny tasting water before hurrying back down the stairs to her cot. As before the light winked off, flooding the basement with darkness. Squeezing her eyes closed, she wrapped the blanket around her and scrunched into a ball to keep warm.

Sobs caught in her throat. She swallowed them. They did no good. Daddy wasn't coming. She missed her daddy…sister…bro…ther.

Wh-what's…hap…pen…

Suddenly her mind swirled, each thought there for just a second, then gone. She opened her eyes, but they immediately slid closed again.

Day five, 7:30 a.m.: Ashley missing one hundred and nine hours

Seated at J.T.'s table in his kitchen for the second morning in a row, Madison felt the strain in the air among Kim, Neil and J.T. Halfway through day five and they didn't have much to go on. So many clues led to dead ends—like Eric Carlton. No one at the hotel could place the person who had bought him the vacation. They couldn't even tell them if it was a male or female.

Yesterday evening after another prayer vigil at church, they had continued to check out the ex-cons and new people to Crystal Springs. Rachel was still delving into Max Dillard's background, but no good leads yet.

Although he had gotten more sleep last night, J.T.

appeared beyond exhaustion. He was functioning on sheer willpower. "I think you two should go back to school. Keep yourself—"

Neil interrupted. "No way, Dad! I couldn't focus on my classes."

"Me, neither. I'm not going." Kim crossed her arms, a pout on her face.

J.T.'s gaze skipped from one child to the other then back. "You have finals."

"Our teachers understand."

J.T. played with his scrambled eggs, his gaze glued to his food, his movements slow, laborious. Again silence descended. Madison wanted to hug each one. She wanted to give them as much strength as she had. They were unraveling before her eyes. She ached for them, especially J.T. He was used to solving crimes and the most important one he couldn't.

J.T.'s cell phone rang. Everyone lifted their heads and looked toward him as he unclipped it from his belt and put it to his ear.

"Go to Lakeshore Park."

Click.

He froze for a few seconds with the cell plastered against his ear as the mechanical-sounding voice registered on his brain. Then his heart began to pound. His clammy hand holding the phone shook.

Madison's sharp gaze zeroed in on him. "What's wrong?"

He forced himself to take several deep breaths. "That was the kidnapper. He told me to go to Lakeshore Park." J.T. surged to his feet.

"How did he get your cell phone number?" Madison asked.

"It's common knowledge. A lot of people know it. Can you stay with the kids?"

Everyone at the table stood.

"We're going, too, Dad." Neil took a step toward the door.

"Yes, Daddy. We can't sit here waiting to hear from you."

J.T. sent Madison a beseeching look. "I'm coming, too, J.T. We can call for backup on the way."

He dug his keys out of his front pocket, his gaze sweeping over the faces of the others, each set in determination. Frankly, his children were probably safer with him. "Let's go. Madison, you make the necessary calls."

As he sped toward the park near the lake, he questioned the wisdom of bringing his children. What if he found Ashley—dead? The last word shivered through his mind. He had to deal with it now because he couldn't afford to fall apart in front of Neil and Kim. They would look to him for guidance and solace.

Suddenly the real reason he hadn't left them at home struck him. Madison would have had to stay to protect them in case this was a ruse the kidnapper was using to get his other children alone. And he wanted Madison with him—for guidance and solace. It was scary how important Madison had become to him in such a short amount of time.

He pulled into the parking lot near the park entrance with three cars rolling in right after him. When he clambered from his Jeep, he called to Rachel, "I need you to stay with Neil and Kim."

"Dad, I want to come and help look."

"Me, too." Kim gripped the handle to open the back door.

J.T. leaned in. "You two have to stay here. No arguments about this. Do everything Rachel tells you to. Understood?"

Both Neil and Kim nodded somberly.

Neil started to say something. J.T. held up his hand and pinned him with a fierce look. "Don't."

J.T. strode to the group of agents and deputies. Matthew Hendricks directed different teams to fan out from the entrance and scour the park that ran three miles along the north shore of the lake.

J.T., paired with Madison, took the farthest southeast quadrant. He picked his way through the wooded area, comforted by Madison's presence only a few yards away even though they kept quiet to listen for any unusual sounds.

In the distance he spied a mound of blue, not moving. He could have sworn his heart stopped beating for a split second. The pain that ripped through his chest almost drove him to his knees. Fear like a rock anchored in his gut held him immobile for a few seconds.

Then he ran. Ran toward the blue mound. "It's her," he shouted as his legs pumped as fast as they could.

Ten seconds later he fell to his knees beside Ashley, crumpled on the ground at the base of an old oak tree, her back to him. So still. He reached out to feel for a pulse but snatched his hand back, afraid to know the truth.

"Is she alive?" Madison panted next to him.

Lord, let her be alive. Let her be alive. His arm trembled as he stretched it out toward Ashley. *Let her be alive.* He laid two fingers along her warm neck.

He squeezed his eyes closed, whispered, "Thank you, Lord," and turned his daughter toward him. He scooped her up into his arms and held her. Tears gathered in his eyes. He blinked, releasing several to run down his cheeks.

"J.T., look."

He glanced at Madison and followed the direction she was pointing. Then he saw it. A note he must have dislodged when he moved Ashley.

In bold red letters cut from magazines, it read, "This is only the beginning."

Day six, 7:00 p.m.: Ashley found eleven hours ago

Madison entered J.T.'s kitchen and found him standing before the refrigerator with the door open, staring at the contents. But she suspected by the faraway look in his eyes that he wasn't really seeing anything before him.

"J.T.?"

Nothing.

She stepped nearer and with more force said, "J.T."

He jerked around and faced her, slamming the refrigerator behind him. "I didn't hear you come in."

"I know."

"When did you get here?"

"Just now. Neil let me in."

He lounged back against the counter, trying to appear

relaxed, but there was nothing casual about the stiff lines of his body. "I didn't hear the doorbell."

"I didn't ring it. I knocked. I didn't want to wake Ashley up if she was sleeping."

"She's not. She's playing a game with Neil and Kim in the den. They won't leave her side." He peered at the refrigerator. "I came in here to make something for dinner. Or, rather, heat something up. The ladies of the church have been filling my kitchen with food all day long." He swept his arm in a wide arc to indicate the counters with various dishes sitting on them. "I don't think I'll have to cook for a month." Suddenly as though he realized he was chattering, something he never did, he clamped his mouth closed.

"Matthew and two agents have left. Paul Kendall and I are staying to help you with the investigation unless you don't want our help."

He sighed. "Of course I want your help. This time it ended good." His gaze drifted toward the window near the table as though he half expected to see the kidnapper spying in on them.

When he didn't continue, Madison waited until his attention returned to her before saying, "But the threat is there. The lab report came back on the note and pajamas. Nothing was found. No fingerprints. Nothing special about the letters, the glue, the paper nor the pajamas she was dressed in."

"Somehow I'm not surprised. The note only confirms this is someone out for revenge against me. We need to double our efforts on the list of criminals. I thank the Lord that my daughter wasn't sexually assaulted. Putting her in pajamas was certainly an effective way to get to me."

"I won! I won!" Ashley shouted from the den.

Madison glanced toward the doorway into the hall. "I'd like to interview her."

"I already did. She doesn't remember anything except being in a dark—" he inhaled several large swallows of air "—basement on a cot with a scratchy blanket. She doesn't know how she got there or to the park."

"Let me try. She may remember something now."

"Fine. You can stay and eat dinner with us. Then you can interview her afterward. I'm trying my best to make everything as normal as possible." He turned back to the refrigerator and opened it. "If you really want to help me, help me decide what to have for dinner."

"I've got a better suggestion. You go into the den with your family while I put something together. I'll call you all when I'm through." She stepped between him and the refrigerator, the cold air chilling her back.

He didn't leave. He stared down at her. "I don't know what I would have done without your help this past few days. You don't know how much it means to me that you're staying to work on the investigation."

She quirked a smile. "You'd have to drag me away."

He brought his hand up to cup her face. His touch warmed her to the tips of her toes. His gaze held hers for a long moment while he stroked his finger along her jaw. Then slowly he leaned toward her.

Madison's heartbeat kicked up a notch. Her mouth went dry as she anticipated the feel of his lips against hers. She wanted him to kiss her.

"Dad! Dad, Kim's cheating."

Neil's voice, full of laughter, propelled J.T. back a step, his hand slipping away from her. "I'd better go referee. It doesn't take long for things to get back to normal."

Madison watched him leave. She wished that were true. But she knew the ordeal of the past five days would stay with this family a long time. When she had seen Ashley earlier at the medical clinic where she was checked out then here at the house, the little girl acted as if she were putting on a performance for everyone to reassure them she was all right. But Madison glimpsed the terror in the child's gaze when her father wasn't looking. For the first half of the day, she hadn't left J.T.'s side.

Suddenly Madison noticed the cold. She shivered, spinning around to see what the ladies of J.T.'s church had brought for the family to eat. Throwing herself into the task of reheating and putting the food on the table was just what she needed. Then maybe she wouldn't focus on *that* moment with J.T. Even with Ashley's return, how in the world could she see herself and J.T. in any kind of relationship? Brent had hurt her so badly that she didn't want to risk that kind of pain ever again, and J.T. had a lot of baggage beyond the fact that someone was out to destroy him and his family. Besides, she decided that her job gave her the fulfillment she needed. It was much safer emotionally.

Madison pulled a chicken casserole out and stuck it into the oven. Then she went back to the refrigerator, took out the makings of a tossed green salad and found a cutting board and a large wooden bowl.

Pausing next to the sink, she grazed her fingertips across her lips. What would his kiss feel like? Probably dynamite! Suddenly she shook her head. *Can't think about that. Best if I never find out.*

She turned her full attention to chopping up a cucumber, some carrots and an avocado for the salad. She was so focused that she jumped when she spied J.T. next to her.

She placed her palm over her heart. "You scared me."

"For the next few hours let's promise each other not to think about the case. This family needs to celebrate. I don't want to ruin this moment for my children."

"Deal." Thankfully he assumed she'd been thinking about the case. There was no way she would tell him he had been the center of her thoughts. Even while dicing the vegetables, she couldn't rid her mind of the dreamy look that entered his eyes as he dipped his head toward her.

"Do you need any help?" He took several sodas from the refrigerator. "Want one?"

"No. You go be with your kids. I won't be long."

As he left, the smile he sent her went straight down her length, making every inch of her tingle. She saw the goose bumps on her arms and was so glad J.T. hadn't. Long ago she had promised herself she would never be attracted to anyone she worked with, especially a partner. It complicated a difficult situation. She knew J.T. wasn't technically her partner and they didn't usually work together, but for the time being she felt they were a team working to solve the case.

What about afterward? an inner voice asked.

Afterward, she would go back to her job in Chicago,

a dream job she had worked hard to get ever since her older brother's killer, a gang member who had driven by and shot at innocent bystanders, had been brought to justice by an FBI agent. Her brother's murder had left a hole in her life that she filled with visions of becoming an agent one day and being there for other families dealing with senseless deaths.

Yes, that was what she needed to concentrate on. Not J.T.'s look or what his kiss might feel like. She'd just gotten her life the way she wanted and that didn't include a man who was a recovering alcoholic.

She stored the finished salad in the refrigerator, then headed for the den to join J.T. and the children until the casserole was heated. For a few hours she would enjoy being part of a family.

Seated around a game table, J.T., Neil, Kim and Ashley were immersed in a wild game of Monopoly. J.T. waved Madison over. "Join us. You can be the banker."

She drew up a chair from the desk. "My kind of job. I like handling the money. A position of power."

Laughter flowed around the table with even Ashley's giggle peppering the air. But being next to the eight-year-old, Madison noticed what no one else saw—the child's tight grip on the side of the chair. When Madison listened closely, she heard the forced lightness in the family's words, especially J.T.'s. Her worry increased. Like Ashley, he was putting up a front for the benefit of his children. But Madison glimpsed the cracks in his armor—a clenched jaw, a narrowed glint, a faraway look, furtive glances toward the window. He had declared no thoughts concerning the case, but his mind wouldn't cooperate if the subdued stress in him was any indication.

"Aha! You owe me big-time!" Neil flipped his deed card over and announced an amount that would bankrupt Kim.

"Daddy, can I borrow some money from you? You're rich."

"Sure." J.T. counted some paper bills and slid them across the table to his middle child.

"Dad, you can't do that!"

"I can do whatever I want with my money, son." J.T. grinned, the gesture actually reaching deep into his eyes.

Madison melted back against the chair. That look, although not for her, caused her stomach to flip-flop. His smile was beautiful, the kind that lit his whole face.

"Yeah!" Kim stuck her tongue out at her brother.

Ashley dropped her head, her gaze glued to her lap. When the room became quiet, she looked up. "Kim, I don't want to play anymore. You can have my money, too." Ashley's whispers could barely be heard.

Instead of taking the money and property, Kim stared at her younger sister, uncertainty in her eyes. "That's okay. I'm getting tired of playing, too."

Madison rose. "Actually I think dinner is ready."

Ten minutes later Madison took a chair between Kim and Ashley, the aroma of the chicken infusing the air with promises of a delicious meal. Everyone linked hands while J.T. said grace, then quickly the dishes were passed around the table.

J.T. and Neil launched into a discussion of Neil's baseball team and their last game coming up that Saturday. Madison tried to follow the conversation, but sports wasn't her thing. When the male agents talked about the different teams they rooted for, it took every effort on her part not to have her eyes glaze over with boredom.

At the end Neil glanced from Ashley to Kim. "I know you two don't like baseball much, but I hope you'll come this Saturday to see me pitch."

Kim groaned and threw a look at Ashley. "I will if you will."

J.T.'s youngest nodded. She drew circles with her fork in the chicken casserole, but Madison noticed the child hadn't taken more than two bites.

Madison sipped her ice water. "Ashley, I can fix you something else to eat if you don't want the chicken." When the little girl didn't say anything but continued to move the food around on her plate, she added, "I saw some peanut butter in the pantry and strawberry jam in the fridge. I could fix you a sandwich if you want."

Ashley's fork clanged to the plate. She raised wide eyes to Madison. "No! No, I hate peanut butter!"

"Honey, since when? You always—"

The child bolted to her feet, the sound of her chair crashing to the floor cutting off the rest of J.T.'s sentence. "I hate it!" Ashley raced from the room.

J.T. shot out of his seat. "Neil and Kim, clean up. I'll see to Ashley."

The helpless look he gave Madison right before he left the kitchen slashed through all her resolve to keep her distance. How could she when he was hurting so badly, when his whole family was?

But, God, what can I do? I have no experience with a family.

TEN

Day six, 8:30 p.m.: Ashley found twelve and a half hours ago

J.T. sat on Ashley's bed, leaning against the headboard, while he held his daughter tightly against him and stroked her back. Her sobs had finally quieted to whimpers, but each sound from her cut him to the core.

He was in over his head. First thing tomorrow he would call Colin and see if he could counsel Ashley. Each word he had tried only increased her cries. In his euphoria that his daughter was home safe and physically unscathed, he neglected the mental anguish she experienced. He knew better, but he had still been focused on bringing the kidnapper to justice, not healing his family. Would he ever learn? Guilt, always there under the surface, reared up and knifed him in the heart.

He was just so tired and spent. Trying to get his family's life back to normal had taken its toll on him— and Ashley. It wasn't normal. And until he caught the man responsible, it never would be. A threat hung over his family. He clamped his jaw tightly together. He would do anything humanly possible to see that threat removed.

"I'm sorry, baby. I'm sorry." He continued to rub his hand up and down Ashley's back.

The whimpering eased. She moved in his arms.

"Tell me what I can do to help you."

Ashley lifted her head from his chest and leaned back to look up at him. Her red swollen eyes proclaimed his inability to protect his family against a monster. Feelings he hadn't had in six years, all tied up in guilt, continued to swamp him, threatening to take him under.

"I prayed—" she sniffed "—for you to come get me."

"Oh, baby, God heard. You're here now, safe." His hand trembling, he combed tear-damp hair away from her face.

"I was…" Her eyes glistened. She sucked in a shallow, shaky breath. "I was…scared. It was so dark and cold."

Something died in J.T. as he listened to his daughter, her tears again streaming down her face. As quickly as he brushed them away, they returned flowing freely. Finally he gave up and pulled her against him, never wanting to release her from the shelter of his arms.

How was he going to do his job when he didn't want to leave her? How was he going to find the monster and make him pay? He needed help.

At that moment he peered toward the open door into Ashley's room and saw Madison framed in the entrance, sorrow in her expression. She entered and sat in the rocking chair a few feet from the bed.

Finally Ashley realized that Madison was there and sat up, drying her face with the back of her hand. His daughter sniffled.

"Hi." Madison smiled, but the corners of her mouth quivered. "I noticed some sugar cookies in the kitchen. Kim told me you love Mrs. Goldsmith's cookies. Would you like them and some milk?"

"Yes, please."

While Madison left to get the food, J.T. took his daughter's face in his hands. "I won't let anything happen to you, Ashley. I'll find the person who did this to you."

When Madison came back into the room, Ashley scooted to the edge near her bedside table where Madison set the plate and drink. The child picked up a sugar cookie and broke it into two pieces. A frown scrunched her forehead as the little girl brought one of the bits to her nose and sniffed it.

Ashley dropped the cookie. "I don't want it. I remember that smell in the basement." She pushed the plate away.

Madison rushed forward and caught the glass before the milk tipped over. She sat next to Ashley. "What do you mean this smells like where you were?"

Ashley tilted her head to the side and screwed up her face in a thoughtful expression. "It reminds me of a smell I smelled when I was eating my last meal." She placed a hand over her stomach, bending forward. "I don't like that smell. Bad. Bad. Bad."

Day six, 11:00 p.m.: Ashley found fifteen hours ago

Later that night J.T. entered his office after saying good-night to Madison an hour ago at his house. The bright overhead light assaulted his tired, burning eyes. After he flipped off the switch, he tugged on the chain to the small lamp on his desk, then pulled closed the blinds to his large picture window. He collapsed into his padded desk chair, the force of the movement rolling it a few inches.

He leaned forward, thankful that Rachel had volunteered to stay at his house while he came down to the station to see if he could make any sense out of the myriad of clues in the case. Who was he kidding? Their various leads pointed to no single person. Not one name leaped off the list as the one who was responsible. He felt like Moses wandering in the desert with no idea his final destination.

With his elbows planted on his desk, he buried his face in his hands. Sleep had evaded him yet again. He couldn't get the sound of his daughter's sobs out of his thoughts. Each one had wrenched him with anguish. He'd let Ashley down. She'd suffered for five days because he couldn't find her. In fact, if the kidnapper hadn't let her go, she would still be with him. That realization shook him to his core.

What good was being a sheriff if he couldn't help his family? Being a law enforcement officer was why his daughter was taken. The monster couldn't seek revenge against him. No, he had to come after his children.

What kind of God condoned this?

The question he'd kept pushed back came unbidden into his mind. It mocked the years he had tried to do everything right. The years he hadn't taken a drink. He desperately wanted one at the moment.

He stared down at his hands that quaked with the

force of his need. One drink to steady his nerves, to help him sleep.

He rose and retrieved the car keys from his pocket. He'd passed the liquor store on his way to the station. He remembered its neon sign beckoning him earlier. If he hurried, he could make it right before it closed.

This is only the beginning. Those words, written by the kidnapper, seared their threat into his brain.

Only one drink.

Hands trembling, he reached for the handle and opened his office door.

Day six, 11:00 p.m.: Ashley found fifteen hours ago

Vanilla! Madison shot up in bed, darkness surrounding her in her motel room. Sugar cookies had a lot of vanilla in them. That was the scent Ashley probably smelled, which meant they might be looking for a woman. At least they needed to consider the possibility.

She tore back the covers and switched on the light. She wanted to take another look at the original list of people whom J.T. had been responsible for putting in prison. She thought she had seen a couple of women's names on the list. Why did they rule them out?

Quickly, she dressed and snatched up her keys. A moment later she started her car and headed for the sheriff's office. Excitement bubbled through her. This might be the break they were looking for. They needed something to point them in the right direction. She didn't associate the scent of vanilla with men. Definitely a woman could be involved.

As she pulled onto Lakeshore Drive, in the distance she noticed J.T.'s Jeep parked in his usual space. He was supposed to get a good night's sleep for the first time in days. Why was he here? He needed to take care of himself better, and she intended to tell him that when she saw him.

As she neared the station, J.T. became visible in his Jeep, sitting behind the steering wheel, his head sagging forward. He should be asleep.

Hurriedly she parked next to him and clambered out of her car. J.T. didn't budge. A sudden alarm prodded her steps to quicken. *Why was he here?*

She rapped on his window. J.T. sat unmoving, staring at an open bottle of whiskey cradled in his lap. He didn't look up at her. Her alarm skyrocketed.

She yanked the door open. "J.T., don't. This isn't the answer."

He blinked, as though he finally realized she was there, and glanced at her. The light from the building underscored his haunted expression.

She leaned in, wanting desperately to snatch the bottle from his grasp, but his fingers were locked about the uncapped liquor. "Talk to me."

His shoulders hunched. With his free hand, he kneaded his neck. "I worked so hard to carve a new life for myself and my family. Six years gone just like that." Raising his gaze, he snapped his fingers. "I hadn't bought a bottle of whiskey in six years, but I did tonight. I haven't taken a drink, but I want to. I *really* want to."

"Did it solve your problems back then or make them worse?"

A bleakness edged its way into his eyes. "Why did God do this to me and my family?"

"First, God didn't do any of this. This was caused by evil." She got into his face, gripping his arm nearest her. "But God will help you through this. Don't shut Him out when you need Him the most. Don't let evil win."

"Madison, do you know what it is like to hold your child in your arms and listen to her cry her heart out? I have never felt so helpless in my entire life. So alone."

"You aren't alone. God is with you. I'm with you." So close their breaths tangled, she rubbed her hand up and down his arm, cold skin beneath her fingertips. "C'mon, let's go for a walk. It's actually very nice tonight." She drew him out of his Jeep.

He peered down at the whiskey, still clutched in his fist.

"If you still want a drink when we get back, then so be it. I won't stop you."

J.T. reached into the vehicle and found the cap. After he screwed it back on the bottle, he placed the liquor in his glove compartment. Then he locked his car and walked to the station.

He poked his head in and said to Derek, "You can reach me on my cell. Call me, especially if it's Rachel." Outside on the sidewalk, he took a deep, lung-filling breath. "Rachel's at my house, watching my kids. I thought I would come down here and work on the case since I couldn't sleep." He sent her a wry grin. "I didn't get very far. Why did you come?"

She linked her hand with his and began strolling toward the park in the center of the town. "The case. I woke up and couldn't go back to sleep so I thought I might get some work done on it." This wasn't the time to discuss the kidnapping. She had something else to fight for: J.T.'s peace of mind.

The near half-moon illuminated his grin. "You and I think a lot alike."

"Yep, it seems so." His hand fit so naturally in hers, as if they had walked like this many times in the past and would in the future. The sensation that she belonged beside him scared her. She was in Crystal Springs temporarily. Her career and life were back in Chicago. "You know what? I can't get over how quiet it is here at night. I'm used to noise, even in the middle of the night in Chicago. How do you sleep?"

The sound of his laughter sprinkled the air like stardust. "I didn't when I first came here. But like most things in life, you get used to a change and you're all right after a time. But that first month I lost a lot of sleep. I was probably as cranky as a grizzly bear after a long winter's nap."

"I know you are countrified if you're talking about wild animals."

J.T. stopped at the edge of the park, near the bench they sat on only days before. "Thankfully there aren't any grizzly bears around here, but we have on occasion seen a black bear."

"I imagine the type of bear wouldn't mean much to me as I'm running for my life." The rumble of his laughter delighted her. "Do you want to sit here and talk?" She pointed toward the bench.

"No, I have a better place. Come with me." He tugged her forward, cutting across the park to the other street.

"Where are we going?"

"Where I should have gone in the first place? You reminded me of that earlier."

When she saw the Faith Community Church up ahead, it all made sense—and it was the perfect place. "You have a key?"

He increased his pace. "Don't need one. The sanctuary is never locked."

Madison came to a dead halt, causing J.T. to stop and look back at her. "Not locked! Are you all mad?"

"I always thought it was sad that we had come to locking up our churches. Doesn't that defeat the purpose of what the church symbolizes—a haven for lost souls in time of need? That lost doesn't happen on a time schedule."

"Beautifully put."

"Those weren't my words. They were Colin's. He's right, though. The first few years I was here I frequented the church late at night while I wrestled with being a single dad and fighting alcoholism." He opened the door for her to enter the foyer. "Although a recovering alcoholic, I'm always aware I'm just one drink away from being a full-fledged alcoholic again."

In the sanctuary J.T. went to the front and sat in the first pew. "In my complacency I forgot how calming this place can be." He let out a long sigh. "It's renewing." He slipped his hand over hers on the seat.

For a few seconds all she could think about was the feel of his palm against her skin, then she opened her mind to the serenity of the church, to God's spirit. Bowing her head, she prayed. *My Heavenly Father, please guide me in helping J.T. Show me the way. He hasn't come this far in his battle to give it all up now.*

After a few minutes of silence, Madison knew she had to broach the subject that had brought them to this place. She wasn't going to let J.T. slip backward without a fight. Memories of what liquor had done to her father stiffened her determination.

"Why did you start drinking in the first place?"

The tightening of his hand transmitted his stress. "It started when I would go out with the guys after work to a bar and have a few to unwind, to forget the ugliness of our job."

"There's more than ugliness in our jobs. There's nothing like the feeling I get when I've helped someone or gotten a criminal off the street so he can no longer hurt anyone."

"I lost the ability to focus on the good, the positive. When I came to God, I was able to change my focus more to that. But—" he shook his head "—this person who wants revenge has brought all those old feelings back. All the guilt."

"Guilt? Over the drinking?"

"More than that. I'm the reason my wife is dead. If I hadn't been drinking, she would be alive today."

His words, uttered in the quiet of the church, rocked her. "Did you drink and drive?"

"No, but we had a big argument about my drinking one evening. She left to walk it off and was hit by a car."

"So if you hadn't been drinking, she wouldn't have been out there walking off her anger? Is that it?"

"Something like that."

"Has your guilt brought her back?"

He frowned. "No, but—"

"Have you confessed and asked God for forgiveness?"

"Yes, but—"

"'If we confess our sins, He is faithful and just to forgive us our sins, and to cleanse us from all unrighteousness.' Do you not believe those words from the book of John?"

"It's not that simple." J.T. stared at the cross hanging from the ceiling over the altar.

"Yes, it is. Turn your guilt over to the Lord. Let Him wash you clean of it. This is the time you need your faith more than ever."

"I'm trying." He looked at Madison. "You know what Ashley said to me tonight? She's worried the bad man will come get her again. So am I. He's toying with me. Has been all along."

She maneuvered around so she faced him on the pew. "You can't let this person win."

He smiled. "I'm glad I have you on my side. You've been my anchor through all this."

"And God?"

"Yes, but I still don't understand why something like this happened to Ashley. She's so innocent."

"You know more than most people that bad things happen to good people. No guarantees in this life, only the next one. But God has given you what you need to weather the storm. Your kids are blessed to have you."

"I won't let that monster win. I won't let him harm another one of my children."

"What if it isn't a him?"

J.T. started to say something but stopped and thought a moment, cocking his head to one side as was his habit. "Why do you say that? We ruled out all of the women I put behind bars."

"Tonight I woke up because I figured out the scent that Ashley probably smelled was vanilla. When I think of the scent of vanilla, I think of a woman, not a man."

"Maybe Ashley was intended to smell it. She only smelled it the last time she ate before she was released. What if the person used it to throw us off? I feel that way about most of the leads we've gotten so far."

"That's always a possibility. But I still want to look at women. Look at this from a different angle."

"I trust your judgment. If you think so, then do it. I still think our best bet is the list of felons."

His compliment gave her a warm feeling in the pit of her stomach. That meant a lot to her. "What if it's a wife or girlfriend of someone you put in prison? The revenge angle still holds true."

"That opens up a whole new list."

"I want to work on that. That's why I came down to the station to reassess our search, expand it."

"I can't believe I'm saying this, but tomorrow is soon enough. We both need to get some sleep. I don't know about you, but my mind is getting fuzzy."

"Fine. First thing tomorrow morning I'll start on it."

He lifted the hand that he held and sandwiched it between his. "Thank you."

Their gazes connected, and the bond that had formed from the very beginning blossomed. J.T.'s eyes blazed, and his intense regard took in her features as though he were memorizing them.

He cradled her face with one hand, never taking his eyes from hers. "Thank you isn't adequate for what I feel. There were times I felt everything was coming apart and I would look at you working so hard to find Ashley. You gave me hope and what I needed to keep going."

He pulled her into his embrace and just held her against him. His aftershave teased her senses. The feel of his arms about her sent a wave of contentment through her. What was happening to her? Surely these feelings were because their emotions were so intense concerning the case. She did not want to be hurt again. She did not want to mistake this for something it wasn't.

When he leaned away and caught her gaze, he ran his thumb over her lips. Those heightened emotions jammed her throat and made it difficult to say anything. Although his thumb was rough, his touch was so gentle it tingled.

"If we're gonna get any rest, we'd better leave." J.T. rose and tugged her to her feet.

He headed toward the entrance into the sanctuary, his hand joined with hers. Out in the foyer he stopped and drew her against him, gliding his fingers through her hair. His mouth met hers in a searing kiss.

For a long moment as he held her against him, she'd felt as though she'd come home. That sensation panicked her, startling her in its intensity. When had he become so important to her?

When they parted, he rested his forehead against hers, his hands cradling her face. "I have wanted to do that since last summer."

Then without another word he walked out of the church with his arm around her shoulders so that her body pressed along his side. They moved as one back toward the sheriff's office.

The warm breeze teased her hair. The scent of honeysuckle from along one side of the church sweetened the air. Stars glittered in the dark sky, vying with the moon for dominance. A perfect evening. But she knew that evil still lurked in Crystal Springs. She shivered.

"Cold?" He brought her even closer as if he could protect her.

"No, just thinking about what needs to be done."

J.T. came to a stop at Madison's car in front of the station. "Come by and have breakfast with us tomorrow morning. That's the least I can do for all your help. My kids enjoy having you."

Just your kids? "What time?"

"Seven."

"You cooking again?"

"I thought I would get you to help me." He wiggled his eyebrows.

She laughed. "I'm thinking you are the better chef, but if you're game, I'll help." She lounged back against her car. "What about the kids tomorrow?"

"I want them to go back to school, at least Neil and Kim. I think the quicker we get back into a normal routine the better for everyone. Neil graduates next Monday and there's only a few days of school left for Kim."

"What about Ashley?"

"Colin has been counseling Kim and Neil and will continue to, but I want him to start with Ashley tomorrow. She's scared to be alone. I don't want her to feel I've abandoned her at school. I want to get her whatever kind of therapy she needs."

"Time hopefully will help her."

"Time and us finding the kidnapper."

"We will." They had to. It was so hard seeing people she cared about in so much pain.

"I think Neil and Kim will be all right at school. They know to be careful." He rubbed his thumb along her lips. "I have something for you."

He moved to his Jeep, unlocked it and removed the whiskey. When he came back to her, he uncapped the bottle and poured it down the sewer in the street. "This won't help me solve my problems. Thanks for reminding me of that and that God was there for me six years ago and is here for me now."

Having lived with a father who would never have done that, she was thrilled by his actions. Madison grinned her thanks at him, then turned to open her car. "See you at seven."

J.T. halted her movement, twisting her back toward him. He kissed her hard and quick. "Good night."

When she slipped behind the wheel, her hands trembled as she gripped it. That kiss took her by surprise—a pleasant one. She brushed her fingers across her lips, remembering the feel of his mouth against hers. Wow!

When J.T. settled himself in his Jeep, she started her engine and backed out of the parking space, then followed J.T. down Lakeshore Drive until she came to her motel. He honked as she turned into her temporary residence.

Tomorrow she would compile a new list with the focus on women. The possibility couldn't be ruled out and up until now they hadn't really considered the kidnapper being anything but a man. They had to look at every angle. Time was their enemy. The kidnapper could strike again. She felt something would happen soon.

Day six, 1:00 p.m.: Ashley found seventeen hours ago

J.T. paused in the open doorway to Ashley's room. Both of his daughters lay curled next to each other on the double bed, Kim's arm thrown over her younger sister as though protecting her. The picture thickened his throat.

Rachel sat in the rocking chair near the bed. When she saw him, she rose and strode toward him. "She wouldn't go to sleep until Kim and I stayed in the room."

"Thanks, Rachel. I know you, in fact everyone, are going above and beyond your job description." J.T. stepped into the hallway.

"My job is to keep the citizens of this county safe and that's what I'm doing. I told you to call me anytime. I know you don't want to leave them alone, yet you have things that you need to do. Did you come up with any leads?"

"Actually Madison thinks we should look at women, as well."

"We ruled out the ones you put in jail."

"Maybe it's someone connected with one of the men I sent to prison."

Rachel whistled low. "That will open a new direction."

"We'll work on it tomorrow. I'll be in after I get the kids off to school. I'm bringing Ashley to work with me. I don't think she's ready to go back to school."

"You're probably right."

After Rachel left, J.T. entered his daughter's bedroom again and eased into the rocking chair. He'd come close to losing it tonight. He'd made the decision before Madison had arrived not to take a drink, but her presence had reinforced his need to stay sober, not to slide back into that old life that nearly destroyed him and his family.

As he watched his daughters sleep, his heart swelled with love. Before he'd gone to the station, he'd been weary, frantic and desperate because it looked as if there was no end to the nightmarish threat hanging over his family. He didn't feel that way anymore. Yes, he was still weary, but the desperation was gone. Calmness flowed through him. Madison had reminded him of what was the most important thing in his life: God.

J.T. knelt next to Ashley's bed, closed his eyes and opened his heart. He had been tested and survived. He hadn't taken that drink. "Thank You, Lord, for being there for me. Thank You for bringing my daughter home and thank You for Your love and guidance. Your power has strengthened me even beyond what I had thought I was capable of. Six years ago I wouldn't have been able to deal with this crisis. I would have lost myself in a bottle. Not this evening. You were there with me as You always have been. For a moment I forgot. Thank You."

He rested his head on the mattress. Through his exhaustion hope shone. He would find the person responsible for Ashley's kidnapping. He wouldn't let anyone hold his family hostage, physically or emotionally.

"Daddy, you're home." Ashley touched his hair.

He looked up. "Hi, honey."

Her eyelids fluttered closed. "Good. You'll stay with me?"

He came to his feet and kissed her on the cheek. "Yes. I'm going to stretch out on the floor next to your bed."

His daughter didn't answer him as she drifted back into sleep. Although he would be getting her counseling, J.T. knew that she would be all right with time. God was with her.

ELEVEN

Day six, 9:00 a.m.: Ashley found twenty-five hours ago

Seated at her usual table at the station the next morning after sharing breakfast with J.T. and his family, Madison finished reading a report and shuffled it to the bottom of her huge stack. She was reviewing all the evidence, keeping in mind a woman could be the kidnapper. Her gaze lit upon the next one from Kirk about the metallic blue car. Since the vehicle's discovery was old news, she started to ignore it when the deputy's description of the Chevy caught her attention. No tinted windows.

She thought back a few days to her interview with Mrs. Goldsmith. Something was wrong. Madison dug through her reports until she found Ruth's the day after Ashley's kidnapping. J.T.'s neighbor had said the reason she hadn't seen the person driving the metallic blue car was because the windows had been tinted dark, but they weren't. A mistake on Ruth's part or a lie?

Madison leaned against the table, her palm supporting her chin. Something else nagged her. What? Closing her eyes, she tried to go back over the interview in her mind, picturing the whole scene. She was on the couple's porch, waiting for someone to open the door. She turned to scan the street. She saw the reporters, the people hurrying toward the staging area of the search, the white car in the Goldsmiths' driveway.

A white car! That was it! Coupled with the discrepancy in the description of the metallic blue vehicle and even the time frame of the kidnapping, it was enough to prompt Madison to write Ruth's name on her list of people to check out.

Then another memory flashed into her mind. The scent of vanilla had permeated the Goldsmiths' house when she had gone inside that morning. The woman had been baking sugar cookies. Madison put a star by J.T.'s neighbor's name.

A movement out of the corner of her eye caught Madison's attention. She looked toward J.T. approaching. The tension in his face had eased some after getting a good night's sleep. Madison was glad at least one of them had rested well because throughout the night before all she could think about was his kisses.

He slipped into the chair across from her and smiled. His look melted her insides. It took all her willpower to keep herself sitting upright. Again the sensations his kisses had generated the evening before swamped her.

"Did you discover something?"

J.T.'s question forced her to concentrate on the case, not her attraction to the man. She blinked, pushing herself back against the hard slats of her chair. "How long have the Goldsmiths lived in Crystal Springs?"

A frown chased away the lively gleam in his eyes. "I think they moved here about two-and-a-half years ago. Why?"

"It's probably nothing but Ruth said the windows on the metallic blue car were tinted. They weren't. She also said she saw it pull away at five-forty. The teen driving said he fled the area at six o'clock because the news had come on his radio station." She clasped the arms of the chair. "And the Goldsmiths' own a white car."

"Along with thousands of others. They have been good to my family. I can't see either one of them involved in kidnapping Ashley."

"I smelled vanilla when I interviewed Ruth. She's known for her sugar cookies. Remember Ashley's reaction to them last night?"

J.T.'s frown deepened. "It just can't be her."

"I didn't say it was, but I'm going to check them out thoroughly. Where they came from. Do they have a connection to one of the criminals you put away?"

J.T. raked his hand through his hair. "I hate this. I have to suspect my friends and neighbors."

"While you and your staff work on the list of felons and any females connected with them, Paul and I will look into some of the people in Crystal Springs, not just the ones who have only been here for a short time. If I discover anything, I'll tell you. Otherwise you don't have to be involved."

"Who are you starting with?"

"The people you work with."

J.T.'s eyebrows slashed downward. "My deputies? They were subjected to an in-depth background check before coming to work here. I can't see how there could be anything in their pasts."

"But people like Susan and Elizabeth aren't subjected to a thorough background search. We'll recheck your deputies to rule them out, but I agree with you."

J.T. glanced toward his office with the blinds up and the door open. Inside, Ashley sat at his desk drawing. "Colin will be here shortly to talk with her. I hate thinking someone my daughter knows wanted to hurt her."

"But the person didn't hurt her. Why?"

J.T. swung his gaze back to Madison. "You think that's important?"

"Could be. The felons you described to me wouldn't have thought twice about hurting Ashley. But she was released unharmed and you were told where to find her."

"Some mental game he's playing with me?"

"Maybe. And another thing. The deputy you depend on the most happens to be gone for a two-week vacation at the time of the kidnapping. A coincidence? I don't think so." More and more Madison felt there was a personal association between the kidnapper and J.T.

"You go in your direction while we go in ours. I'm also looking into Max Dillard and any connection to the criminals on my list."

"The FBI agents in New Jersey are still checking into the hotel where Eric Carlton stayed."

He folded his arms on the table and bent forward. "Neil wanted me to see if you would come to his last game tomorrow."

"He's pitching?"

J.T. nodded. "I'd like you to come. As crucial as solving

this case is, I also recognize how important it is to have some time away from it. Kim and Ashley are coming. They wanted me to talk you into it, too. My children have made it clear they like having you around. So do I."

She rarely blushed but her cheeks burned. "A family outing. I'd like that. Did you say Neil graduates next Monday evening?"

"Yes."

"I'd like to see that, too."

"You've got yourself a date then."

Date! The word flew through her mind, setting off fireworks. Since Brent, she hadn't dated more than a few times. She realized J.T. didn't mean it as a real date, but the thought warmed her. What would a real date be like with J. T. Logan?

Day eight, 4:00 p.m.: Ashley found eighty hours ago

Dressed in jeans, a short-sleeved light blue shirt and sandals, Madison lifted her face to the sun. A perfect day at the ballpark. Not a cloud in the sky. A light breeze kept the temperature cool enough to be pleasant and the best part of the day was that she sat next to J.T. with Ashley on his other side next to Kim.

Neil came out onto the field, heading for the pitcher's mound. He had a no-hitter going in the eighth inning. Thanks to J.T.'s explanation she knew how rare a no-hitter was, and with each strike Neil pitched, she was on her feet cheering as loud as J.T. Even Ashley and Kim were excited as they devoured hot dogs, sodas and potato chips.

Neil tossed a few pitches as the first batter came out

of the dugout and walked to the plate. Madison tensed. There were still two more innings and the odds weren't in Neil's favor, but it was about time the Logan family had something good happen.

"Strike one," the umpire shouted.

The next pitch flew over the home plate. The batter swung and missed.

"Strike two."

Madison held her breath as Neil eyed the batter. J.T. covered her hand that lay between them on the bleachers. Neil wound up and threw the ball. It sailed toward the batter who stepped into it. The crack of the bat against the ball sounded in the sudden quiet of the park. The ball popped up. Neil backpedaled while the batter ran toward first. J.T.'s grip tightened.

When his son caught the fly, Madison leaped to her feet at the same time as J.T., yelling and pumping their linked hands into the air.

J.T. swung around, scooped Ashley into his arms and hugged her. "Neil's gonna get a no-hitter. I can just feel it."

His daughter giggled. "Daddy, you're funny."

J.T. slanted a look toward Madison. "I don't think my daughter appreciates the significance of a no-hitter."

"Sure I do, Daddy. It makes you happy."

J.T. smiled. "It sure does, pumpkin."

Through the rest of Neil's successful inning with not one hit, J.T.'s presence next to Madison heightened her senses. The aromas of popcorn and hot dogs vied with the scent of the recently mowed field behind the ball-park. Everything from the green grass and trees to the azure-blue sky seemed sharp, clear, the colors more vivid than usual. The brush of his arm against her magnified her reaction to him. Her heart beat faster. Her breathing became shallower.

"This is it. The last inning," J.T. whispered close to her ear.

Her neck tingled from the featherlight touch of his breath as he spoke. She trembled.

"Cold?" One of his eyebrows rose.

The mischievous expression in his eyes told her he knew exactly what he was doing to her right here in front of half of Crystal Springs. Too much more and she would dissolve into a puddle of Jell-O left out on a hot summer's day.

She leaned near. "Turnabout is fair play." She blew on his neck and grinned when a tremor passed down his body.

His laugh that followed spiced the air, prompting Madison's smile to widen. "Touché. That's one of the things I like about you."

Those words caused Madison to float halfway through the last inning, not aware of much that was happening on the field. By the time she'd forced her concentration back to the game, Neil faced the last batter if he managed to strike him out. Vaguely she wondered if Neil still had a no-hitter. She thought he did from all the cheering going on around her.

When he pitched three straight strikes and the fans erupted into wild cheers, Madison got her answer. Neil had his no-hitter. J.T. jumped to his feet, taking her up into his arms and planting a kiss on her mouth. Then he swung around and hugged Ashley and Kim.

Stunned, Madison stared at J.T. with his daughters. The urge to touch her lips was so strong she had to clench her hands to keep from doing that.

"We are gonna celebrate tonight. We have so much to be thankful for." J.T. shifted back toward Madison. "How about going with us on a picnic at the park along the lake?"

"I'm game." To spend a few hours not thinking about the case sounded wonderful to Madison. She was beginning to feel she was too close to the facts to see what was missing.

The more she delved into the people in Crystal Springs the more she realized some of them had something to hide. She hadn't been able to discover what Ross Morgan had done as a teenager because his juvenile records were sealed, but she had an FBI agent interview some people who had known him while he was in high school. She found out Ross had been caught stealing from his neighbors. What else was he capable of doing to his neighbors?

There was also Howard Wright, one of Neil's baseball coaches, who'd had ties to a porn site on the Internet a few years back before coming to Crystal Springs. Charges had been filed but later dropped. Why? How far had the man gone in his interests? Had it extended to little girls? He was definitely someone to watch. Howard always wore cowboy boots to remind him of his home state. He even had them on while coaching Neil's team.

Madison scanned the fans in the bleachers. What other secrets would she uncover? These were J.T.'s friends, yet one of them could be the kidnapper. She couldn't shake that feeling as she investigated the townspeople. The more she uncovered, the more she felt this.

"Ready?" J.T. grasped Ashley's hand. "We've got enough food back at the house to invite the whole town on a picnic." When a frown appeared on his youngest daughter's face, he quickly continued, "But we won't. I want you all to myself."

Ashley beamed. "Can we take our fishing poles?"

"Sure, pumpkin. We haven't done that yet this year. That sounds like a good idea."

"Yuck. Fishing." Kim screwed up her face. "I'm not eating anything you catch."

Ashley made a face at her older sister. "You don't have to. Daddy will."

Kim started toward the center aisle with Ashley right behind her. "Good. Just wanted to make that clear."

J.T. peered back at Madison. "Now this is what I'm used to. Their bickering is music to my ears. I can't believe I'm saying that."

"Colin's talks seem to be helping Ashley."

"I slept in her room again on the floor last night, but she only woke up once with a bad dream. Better than the night before."

"You know what they say about time healing all wounds."

He turned back to her. "I hope so. It's hard watching my child in pain."

"Dad, I'm hungry." Kim stood at the end of the row with her hand on her hip.

"Me, too, Daddy." Ashley mimicked her older sister.

J.T. chuckled. "I guess we'd better get moving."

After gathering Neil and stopping at the house for a basket full of food and the fishing gear, J.T. pulled into the parking lot next to the entrance of the lakeside park. At first Madison thought they were going to the same one where Ashley had been found a few days before, but this park was on the other side of Crystal Springs. She noticed a beach where people could swim and a pier near the sandy shore.

The temperature hovered in the high seventies. The breeze blew off the lake, causing a few whitecaps. Several speedboats passed them. One person waved. For a moment Madison thought about the evening of the botched ransom drop. For some reason she felt the object of the ransom demand hadn't necessarily been money.

Why had Max been killed? They finally discovered where he had worked before coming to Central City. He had been a cook at Goldie's Grill in southern Illinois, a few hours away. She still felt Max was the best lead they had so far.

"Hey, quit thinking about the case." J.T., carrying the food basket, stopped next to her. "Remember we're gonna have some fun for a change."

"How did you know?"

He touched the area right above her eyes. "Your face scrunches up right there when you are in deep thought."

Neil took Ashley's hand and headed for the pier with the fishing gear. Kim hung back by the beach.

When all his children were out of earshot, Madison looked at him. "We should talk about what we found out today. We haven't had a chance to brief each other."

"Later. Ashley needs this. I need this."

He was fully being a parent, and she was glad. During the abduction she worried that he couldn't let go of being the sheriff. "Surely if you can do it, I can."

"It isn't easy, but Colin stressed to me how important it was for us to spend some special time as a family to help replace Ashley's bad memories with good ones. Actually it's not only Ashley's bad memories. We've all had a hard time lately."

She settled her hand on his arm. "You aren't alone."

"I know." He faced the lake, watching Neil bait Ashley's hook. "You don't know how important your presence is to me. When I saw you that first night, I felt the cavalry had arrived."

She laughed. "I've never been referred to as the cavalry."

"It was a compliment."

"I know." She slid a smile toward him as Kim ambled out onto the pier and sat next to her younger sister while Ashley fished. "Where do you want to set up the picnic?"

J.T. gestured to a table under a large maple tree near the water. "Have you ever gone fishing?"

"Nope and I'll leave it to you and your family."

"Where's your sense of adventure?"

"I'm with Kim. Fish smell and they are slimy."

While Madison spread the tablecloth over the flat stone top, J.T. opened the basket and began taking out the food. "I can't get over how generous everyone has been. I had to put some of the dishes in the freezer. There is no way we could eat it all before some of it went bad."

"You're lucky to have such good friends." She hadn't lived in any one place for that long since she left the neighborhood she grew up in.

He swept his gaze toward Ashley and for a second thunder entered his expression. "If you're right, one of those friends could be my daughter's kidnapper."

The pain in his features was fleeting but piercing. She hurriedly said, "J. T. Logan, I thought you were the one who said the case was off-limits, at least for a few hours."

He held up his hands, palms outward. "You got me there."

The crestfallen look that passed over his face produced her laugh. "We have it bad."

"What do you mean?" He finished placing the last item, a chocolate pie, out on the stone table.

"Our work consumes us."

"I think it's part of what makes us good officers. It's not a nine-to-five job."

"Working for the FBI was something I wanted to do for a long time. What part of the job do you like the best?"

J.T. eased down on the bench so he could watch his children. "That's easy. Helping others."

"I like that, too, but I also like solving puzzles. I used to do crossword puzzles as a teen. I loved finishing the one in the *New York Times* every Sunday."

"In ink?"

She spun toward him. "You, too?"

He nodded while Ashley's giggle floated to them. His smile grew to encompass his whole face. "That's a beautiful sound."

"None better." She sat next to him, so close their sides touched.

His nearness seeped deep into her heart as they both stared at his three children on the pier, Neil standing up and fishing while Kim was seated next to Ashley, who had her pole in the water. Over the edge of the pier Kim swung her legs back and forth lazily, her head bent toward her younger sister while she listened to Ashley tell her something.

"That's a Kodak moment. Where is my camera when I need it?"

The humor in J.T.'s voice added to the intimacy of the moment. For a few minutes Madison could imagine them as a family, on an outing, as if nothing was wrong, as if no one was after him and his children. What would it be like to be a mother? At the age of thirty-two time was flying by her.

"I gave up taking pictures years ago when all I did was put the photos into a drawer never to look at them again."

The light breeze scattered J.T.'s chuckle. "I have a few drawers stuffed with photos, too. Maybe I can convince Kim that scrapbooking is the best hobby she could take up."

"Go for it. It might work."

"I doubt it."

"Daddy," Ashley yelled, scrambling to her feet, "I've got a bite."

J.T. rose and hurried toward his daughter. "I need that camera!"

Madison followed at a more sedate pace and arrived to see Ashley pulling in a foot-long, silvery fish. Her smile split her face, her eyes lit with pleasure.

"This is a fine crappie, pumpkin." J.T. took it off the hook and put it into the bucket of lake water next to Neil. "We can have it tomorrow night for dinner."

"Yuck. You all can. I'm not." Kim wrinkled her nose.

"That's okay. I'll eat it all." Ashley put her pole down on the pier. "I'm hungry, Daddy. Can we eat?"

"Sure." J.T. put his hand on his youngest child's shoulder and walked toward the picnic table.

Neil picked up the fishing gear. "I doubt we'll do much more." He glanced toward the western sky. "It'll get dark soon. Get the bucket, Kim."

Kim eyed the bucket, said, "You get it," and stalked off the pier.

Neil sent Madison an exasperated look. "She's up one moment and down the next."

"It's called hormones. Well, and the yuck factor. But I'll get it for you."

"Thanks."

Madison slowed her pace to keep the water from sloshing out. As she neared the end of the wooden planks, she stopped and adjusted her grip to get a better one. Before stepping off the pier, she surveyed the park. Although the sun, low in the sky, still warmed the air, she shivered. Again she scanned the area, imagining someone behind each tree watching them. She couldn't shake the sensation as she covered the space between her and J.T.

He gave her a smile, saw something in her expression, even though she tried to conceal her concern, and looked around. Anxiety leaked into his gaze.

He pushed his worry away as he faced his children, handing each one a ham sandwich. "Eat up. We'll have the pie back at the house. When I brought it, I didn't think about how messy it would be."

Madison slipped in beside him on the bench, the hairs on her neck standing straight up. "Well, in that case, let's hurry. That chocolate pie looks delicious." She forced a cheerful tone so she wouldn't scare the kids, all she wanted to do was pull her gun and search the park.

Day eight, 9:00 p.m.: Ashley found eighty-five hours ago

"We've got church tomorrow so I don't want you watching TV too long. I'll be in the kitchen helping Madison clean up." J.T. boxed up the board game they had been playing, put it on the shelf and headed toward the den door.

He paused and peered back at his family. Kim and Ashley settled on the couch and began watching a movie while Neil sat at the desk and made a call. The incident at the park earlier in the evening only reaffirmed the urgency in finding who was behind Ashley's abduction. There would be nothing normal about their lives until that happened. Whether the kidnapper had been watching him and his family wasn't really the point. In his mind it was as if they were being held captive by the unknown threat.

Entering the kitchen, J.T. found Madison standing by the sink, wiping it down. "Did I time it right?"

She swung around, her eyes twinkling with humor. "If you mean am I through cleaning up, then yes, you timed it just right. What are the kids doing?"

"They wanted to watch a movie."

"Which gives us some time to talk about earlier."

He nodded and moved toward the kitchen table. He

pulled the blinds by it and sat. "You think he followed us to the park?"

"Maybe. I don't know. It felt like someone was watching us. I know your deputies we called didn't find anyone when they searched, but still…"

She laid the washcloth over the middle hump in the sink. "I could have been overreacting to a shift in the wind or something."

"No, I felt it, too. Someone was out there. Which means my children aren't safe. I can't take any chances. I'm keeping Ashley out of school this last week. It's only a few days until the end. She'll stay at the station with me and I'll have a deputy go with Neil and Kim. Neil only has one more day. The seniors get out of school earlier than the others. He can help down at the station, too."

Madison eased herself into the chair next to J.T. "That would probably be wise. We need to meet with Paul tomorrow and review all the evidence we've discovered so far. There's got to be something we're not seeing. Paul has some leads to finish up this evening so maybe he'll know more by then."

"Yeah, I have Rachel working on some information on the women in each of the felon's lives. We had to go back to the original list, but she should have it completed by then."

Madison leaned against the table, her arms on its top. "Maybe I'll stop by the station on the way to the motel. See if Paul needs any help. He was waiting on a couple of faxes."

J.T. covered her hand with his. "We needed this

evening. This case has consumed us 24-7 for the past week. As I remember someone telling me not too long ago, we have to take some time for ourselves if we're going to be worth anything in this investigation. Come to church with us tomorrow morning, then I'll see if Kirk can stay with my children while we have the powwow with Paul in my office."

"That would be nice. I love spending time with your family." She dropped her gaze to their linked hands.

"Just my family?"

"Spending time with a certain sheriff isn't bad, either."

Her words produced a burst of elation in the midst of the horror of the past week. *Lord, what is happening to me?* After his failed marriage with Lindsay, he'd never imagined having a second chance at love, but the feelings developing with Madison certainly resembled love.

All the reasons why this wasn't a good time to fall in love engulfed him. He slipped his hand away from Madison's, and disappointment glinted in her eyes before she masked it.

She rose, an emotional barrier now firmly in place. "I'd better be going."

"To the station?"

She gathered her purse from the counter. "I won't stay long. I just want to check and see if those faxes came in. Truthfully I'm so tired I probably wouldn't be able to make any sense out of them anyway." She started for the front of the house.

J.T. pursued her, finally catching up with her on the porch. He grasped her arm to still her flight. "Madison?"

She peered back at him, her gaze lowering to his

hand on her. "I know this isn't a good time for us. There probably isn't a good time for us. I live in Chicago with a job I really enjoy. You live here. Crystal Springs is perfect for you and your family."

"But not you?" No matter how much he rationalized, he couldn't seem to stay away from her.

She sighed. "I don't know. I'm not sure I understand what is happening between us."

J.T. stepped close, invading her personal space, his hands framing her face. "I care about you, more than I should at the moment. My energy and focus must be on protecting my family."

"Of course. And so should mine. I don't want anything to happen to your children. They've come to mean a lot to me."

Her words soothed some of the pain. He wanted to care for her freely, but he might never be able to. Even if the kidnapper was caught, how could he ask her to give up her FBI job, her dream, and live in Crystal Springs? He knew he could never live in Chicago again. There were too many bad memories to build a new relationship there.

"I'm glad we had this evening," he whispered right before claiming her lips in a gentle kiss meant to communicate.

Her arms wound about him, her body pressed against his as though chilled and seeking warmth. She had been by his side every step of the way, supporting him through a nightmare he hoped never to relive.

When he tugged away and put a few feet between them, his ragged breathing sounded in the quiet, matching hers. He couldn't see her expression, but he sensed the profound effect their kiss had on both of them.

"Good night, J.T."

She spun around and hastened down the steps. She climbed into her car and pulled away from the curb in front of his house. He watched her drive away until she turned the corner and her taillights disappeared in the dark.

J.T. started to go back into his home when that sensation of being observed deluged him as if someone had thrown a icy bucket of water, freezing him solid. Tremor after tremor rippled through him.

The watcher, filled with hate, zeroed in on J.T. standing on his porch searching the dark shadows.

Soon, J.T. An eye for an eye.

TWELVE

Day nine, 1:00 p.m.: Ashley found one hundred and one hours ago

After church on Sunday, Madison entered J.T.'s office with her notes on the case. Paul came in right behind her, pulling the door closed. J.T. looked up from reading a paper and motioned for them to sit in the two chairs in front of his desk.

"I'd like us to meet every day until we solve this. Go over anything we've discovered even if we think it's not important." J.T. straightened the stack in front of him, then took the first stapled sheets from the top. "Rachel finished compiling the list of white cars in the area. As you'll see the list is long." He cocked a grin. "I knew white was a common color but not this common."

Madison grabbed the papers that J.T. handed her across his desk. "There are thousands of names on here." She gave Paul his own list.

"It includes Central City since it's less than an hour

away. Rachel's name as well as Ted's is on the list. She has an old white Cougar. Ted has a Ford Focus." J.T. flipped through his copy. "At this point I'll have Rachel mark anyone on here that she knows or has seen on one of our other lists. Otherwise we'll use it as a reference when a new name pops up."

"Sounds good." Madison placed the stapled papers at the bottom of her stack. "You know what we've found out about Howard Wright. He didn't come up on the sex offender list because he was never convicted of anything, but he definitely needs to be watched."

"And interviewed." J.T.'s jaw clenched, his hand balling into a fist on the desk. "I want to do that. He's my son's baseball coach. I'll pay him a visit this afternoon after our meeting."

"I'd like to come along." Madison peered down at the next name on her paper. "Paul just verified this. Susan Winn has holes in her history."

J.T. leaned forward, his eyes wide. "She does?"

"She doesn't match the age she should be according to her Social Security number."

J.T. swung his gaze to Paul. "I want to be here when you talk to her. Any other red flags so far?"

"All your deputies check out. But Elizabeth's husband was in prison," the male FBI agent said.

"Did I put him away?"

"Not that I can tell, but he was in the same prison with some of those names on your list."

"Is he out?"

"Yeah, and living in Chicago."

"I wonder why they aren't together if they are still married.

"It's worth checking into." J.T. massaged the back of his neck. "I can't imagine what her reason for kidnapping Ashley would be, but we can't overlook anything."

"I haven't found anything else on Ross Morgan except the information about his juvenile record. But there is something else interesting. His wife isn't where she's supposed to be. Jill isn't at her parents. They haven't heard from her and aren't expecting her. Ross keeps insisting that's where she said she was going. He wants to fill out a missing person report on her." Madison shifted in her chair, crossing her legs.

"The concerned husband now?" J.T. picked up his pen and scribbled something on a notepad.

"He's coming in later." Madison rose.

Paul stood, too. "I'll take his statement."

J.T. withdrew his car keys from his pocket. "Call him and have him come in now. We're going to see Howard. Then after Ross leaves, bring Elizabeth in then Susan. We should be back by then for those two interviews."

Out in the main room J.T. scanned the area as though seeing it for the first time. With a deep sigh, he headed toward the front door. Outside he stopped by his Jeep and said. "It's hard to believe someone I know is responsible for what's happening. I want these people ruled out first."

Madison slipped into the passenger seat at the same time J.T. got into the car. "Suspecting your neighbors makes this case doubly hard, but we have to look into everything."

He sent her a grim look. "I know. Elizabeth, Susan, the Morgans, the Goldsmiths and even Rachel because of her car. I'm glad we can at least rule Ted out since he's on vacation. It's hard to believe any of them capable of kidnapping." J.T. threw his Jeep in Reverse and backed out of the parking space. "But Howard is another story. To think he was involved in porn."

"He never went to trial. We need to hear his side."

"Right now what I'm feeling isn't very nice."

"So you're gonna be the bad cop in this interview."

He chuckled. "Definitely."

Ten minutes later J.T. parked in front of a large red-brick, two-story house on an acre piece of property. Madison walked beside J.T. up the stairs to the porch.

"His house is kind of isolated from his neighbors." She pressed the button and heard chimes sounding.

"Yeah, but he doesn't drive a white car."

"The car could have been stolen or a false lead."

"Or what the kidnapper drove."

The door opened as Madison said, "True. It's hard to tell what the truth is anymore."

Howard's gaze skipped from J.T. to her then back to J.T. A frown wiped his greeting from his face. "What's happened?"

J.T. stepped forward. "We need to talk to you. Can we come in?"

Howard's forehead wrinkled. "What is this about?" Then suddenly a light dawned in his eyes. "You found out about Houston."

"We can discuss it here on your front porch, down at the station or in your living room. Which will it be?"

The firmness in J.T.'s voice hinted at his tightly reined control.

Howard pushed the door open and backed away for them to enter. "It isn't what you think."

"And what do I think?"

Howard didn't budge from the foyer. "That I sold pornography. I didn't."

"Then why were you charged?"

At J.T.'s query Howard transferred his weight from one foot to the other. "My ex-wife's brother used my computer—" his eyes moved up and to the right of J.T. "—and downloaded some pictures from a porn site. What he did with them I don't know. I was never convicted."

Tension poured off J.T., and Madison moved slightly in front of him. "May we take a look around? Check out your computer."

Howard stared at her. "No, not unless you have a warrant."

"What do you have to hide?" J.T. came forward, his hand opening and closing at his sides.

Howard backed up, blinking. "Nothing. I am a law-abiding citizen who has a right to privacy."

Silence ruled for a long moment.

Howard skirted around J.T. and opened his front door. "I think it's time for you two to leave. Don't come back unless you have a warrant. This is the United States. A person is innocent until proven guilty. Not the other way around."

"You're correct, Mr. Wright. I just thought you would

want to make this easy on everyone." Madison strode toward the door and paused at the entrance.

J.T. glared at Howard, his hands flexing. "A word of advice. Don't have anything to do with children or teens in this county." He stalked toward the door. "You haven't seen the last of me."

Out on the porch at the top of the steps, J.T. halted and inhaled deep breaths. "Did you see him shifting, blinking, looking up and to the right? He was lying. I'll say it again. I'm glad you were with me. To think he coached my son's baseball team." He shook with anger.

Madison clasped his arm and felt the tightly bunched muscles beneath her palm. "I'm not sure if we have enough to get a warrant, but we need to find a judge who will issue one on what evidence we have and with children at stake."

"You and I both know any porn he has will be gone by then."

"But that's not all we're looking for."

Another deep inhalation and J.T. relaxed. "We need to see if he has a basement with a doggy door in the door leading down to it."

"Let's go see a judge."

Day nine, 3:00 p.m.: Ashley found one hundred and three hours ago

"I was hoping that Howard had a basement with a doggy door, then this nightmare would be over." J.T. climbed from his Jeep in front of the sheriff's office.

"And he didn't have a computer at his house." Madison made her way to the sidewalk.

J.T. faced her, the sun starting its descent in the west behind him. "Which is strange. He's a real estate agent who works a lot from his home. I know he had a computer. What did he do with it?"

"Good question."

"And one I intend to pursue. If he's moved here and is continuing something illegal, I'll get to the bottom of it even if he isn't Ashley's kidnapper."

The force behind his words highlighted his determination to make his county as safe as possible. The people of Crystal Springs were blessed to have someone like J.T. as their sheriff, and she hoped the abductor wasn't one of them.

Madison looked into his gray eyes, a silver gleam glittering in their depths. A lock of black hair fell onto his forehead. She stuffed her hands into her pant pockets to keep from brushing the stray strands back into place. A thought about the case nibbled at her, but for the life of her she couldn't think straight with J.T.'s gaze riveted to hers.

He moved closer, chewing up the little space between them. He lifted his hand to her hair and hooked a strand behind her ear. "We make a good team."

Yes, she felt the same way, but the idea of them teaming up on a more permanent basis wasn't likely. *Remember Brent. You thought he was the right man for you and look what happened. And worse, although J.T. is a recovering alcoholic, he had a drinking problem at one time. Do you want to relive your childhood with your father?*

J.T. curled his fingers around her nape, the gray in his eyes softening. "I enjoyed going to church with you this morning."

The husky tone to his words melted any resistance she had managed to conjure. She leaned closer, slipping her hands from her pockets. "A perfect morning."

One corner of his mouth tilted up. "To be topped off with a lousy afternoon."

Not lousy. I'm with you. "We still have Elizabeth and Susan to interview. Maybe something will turn up."

A shadow darkened his features. "I hope not."

His mouth inched nearer. Her eyelids began to close when the sound of the door opening parted them. Ross came barreling out of the station and halted when he spied them.

The man regarded them. "Neither Jill nor I had anything to do with Ashley's kidnapping. How can you think we are suspects?"

J.T. pivoted toward Ross. "Do you know where your wife is?"

"No." J.T.'s neighbor's gaze didn't waver from him. "I'm worried something happened to her. She told me she was going to her parents to think. That's all I know and the last I heard from her. We may be having problems, but she isn't a kidnapper." He stormed past them to his car.

"He sounds convincing." J.T. shoved his hand through his hair, smoothing the stray lock back into place.

"Yes, but we still need to find Jill. What if something did happen to her?"

"Another disappearance? I hope not. Let's see what

Elizabeth has to say. She should be here by now." J.T. opened the door and held it for Madison, who moved inside.

She saw Elizabeth sitting near the break room, her black purse in her lap, her hands clenched around its straps. She chewed her bottom lip. "She looks nervous."

"Let's find out why." J.T. headed for the woman who cleaned the station. "Elizabeth, I'm glad you could come down here."

"Agent Kendall didn't give me a choice. What's this all about?" Her worried gaze swept from J.T.'s to Madison's.

"Please, let's go in here. We just have a few questions for you." J.T. pointed toward the interview room.

Elizabeth's eyes grew round when she noticed where he wanted to talk to her. "You think I did something wrong?"

Madison came to J.T.'s side. "We would rather not discuss it where everyone can hear."

The cleaning lady scanned the large, open area, her eyes widening even more as they lit upon Derek at the counter and Paul at a computer. She struggled to her feet, her hands quaking as they held her purse clutched in front of her. She hurried into the interview room.

Inside, Madison sat across from Elizabeth and clicked on a recorder. After identifying the people involved, the day and time, she asked, "Was your husband convicted of armed robbery and did he serve seven years in the state penitentiary?"

She nodded once.

"Please speak your answer for the record."

"Yes."

"His name is Lance Billingston?"

"Yes."

"Why are you going by Elizabeth Haney?"

"Because I left him. I don't want my sons to grow up with his name. Haney is my maiden name."

J.T. crossed to the table. "Have you ever heard of Neville Sommers, Timothy Connors or Bobby Johnson?"

Bewilderment marked the woman's expression. "No, should I?"

"They were convicts that served in the same prison as your husband." J.T. set his fists on the table and leaned into it.

Elizabeth sat up straight, her chin coming up a notch. "I made it a point never to have anything to do with my husband's friends who served time."

"So you've heard of one of them?" J.T.'s voice sounded tight with agitation.

Elizabeth looked them both in the eye and said, "No, I haven't."

"Do you have a basement?"

Surprise filled the woman's expression. "Basement? I live in a duplex. There isn't a basement. You're welcome to come look."

J.T. inclined his head. "I'll have Deputy Nelson follow you home and check around if that's okay with you."

Now she looked hurt. "That's fine with me. May I go now?"

"Yes." Madison rose.

When the cleaning lady left, she lounged against the table and waited for J.T. to come back from talking with Derek. Two minutes later, he shut the door.

"That was so much fun. Are you ready to repeat it with Susan?" The savagery in his expression contradicted his words.

"It has to be done, J.T. I know you don't like accusing your neighbors and friends of any wrongdoing, but if they're innocent, they'll understand when this is all over with that you were only doing your job."

"I hope you're right because I have to live with these people." He went out to get Susan.

When the older woman arrived, Madison sat again, noticing that J.T. stayed back by the door with his arms folded over his chest. She could feel his reluctance. This was the part of his job he hated.

After the necessary information for the tape was given, Madison asked, "What is your real name?"

Susan's eyelids fluttered, then she fixed her gaze on her hands entwined on the table. "What do you mean? You know my name. It's Susan Winn."

"That's the one you go by now, but that's not your real name. Your information doesn't check out."

Susan drew in a sharp breath and lifted her eyes, tears glistening in them. "I didn't mean to do anything illegal. I couldn't stay." Wet tracks coursed down her cheeks unchecked.

J.T. pushed away from the door and came closer.

Madison stiffened, almost afraid to ask. "What do you mean you couldn't stay?"

"Ralph, that's my ex-husband, used to beat me. I had to disappear before he killed me." Susan used trembling hands to wipe her face.

"Ralph who?" Her heart going out to the woman,

Madison realized she was discovering things about the people in Crystal Springs she wished she wasn't. She felt as if she opened a Pandora's box.

Susan sniffed. "Ralph Baker. I was Cora Baker before I bought this Susan Winn identity." She turned to J.T. "I'm so sorry I broke the law. I didn't know what else to do. He was a mean man. He broke my jaw and several ribs the last time he put me in the hospital."

"Why didn't you file charges against him? Put him in jail?" J.T. finally spoke, moving to stand next to Madison.

Susan's tears began to flow again. "I was scared. He had powerful friends in town."

"Where?" J.T. sat in the chair next to Madison.

"Bakersville near the border of Kentucky. Please don't let him know I'm here and alive. Please."

The pitiful words twisted Madison's heart. She had seen other battered women, trembling and frightened of their husbands, too. It always made her angry and protective. From the look on J.T.'s face, he felt the same way. "We won't, Susan. Our inquiries will be discreet. I promise you."

"I can drive you home, Susan. You're too upset to drive yourself. You still live in that apartment on First Street?"

Nodding, the older woman opened her purse and withdrew a tissue. "Thanks, J.T. I'll be all right." She dabbed at her cheeks and eyes. "Did you need me for anything else?"

"We can ask you later if there's anything else that comes up." Madison stood and offered to help Susan to her feet.

The older woman waved away her assistance and

rose, put her wet tissue into her purse and snapped it closed, then raised fear filled eyes. "Don't contact the sheriff in Bakersville. He's a good friend of Ralph's."

"I won't. Thanks for letting me know." J.T. strode to the door of the interview room and opened it. After Susan left, he faced Madison. "You work with people for years, and yet you don't really know them. She never said a word."

"Would you? In her mind her survival depended on her keeping quiet. I've seen it too many times before."

"When everything with Ashley is over with, we'll have to address this."

"We'll have Paul go to Bakersville tomorrow and check discreetly into Susan's past. It's about two hours south of here, and while he's down that way, he can look into Max Dillard's last place of employment before he came to Central City. Anderson is a little over an hour from Bakersville."

"Kill two birds with one stone. Sounds good to me."

Derek stuck his head through the open doorway. "Boss, Elizabeth doesn't have a basement. There wasn't anything at her house that raised a red flag to me."

"Thanks. I guess now we need to concentrate on Jill and my list of felons and the women in their lives."

Basement? A vague thought nagged her. What was she missing? She began to pace the small interview room. "There's something we should be doing."

"What?"

Then it came to her. She swept around and said, "Howard Wright is a real estate broker. He may have access to various properties that are vacant. One of them may have a basement and a doggy door."

THIRTEEN

Day ten, 12:00 p.m.: Ashley found one hundred and twenty-four hours ago

Sitting in J.T.'s Jeep on Monday afternoon, Madison sank her teeth into the juicy hamburger from the fast-food restaurant. "These are as good as I remembered them."

"Yeah, people come from Central City to eat at Eddie's Hamburger Joint." J.T. popped a fry into his mouth.

"I wish this morning had gone better." She took another big bite of her sandwich.

"Me, too. It was a good idea, though. Howard had four vacant houses listed in the area. They all had basements but not like Ashley described."

"Which probably rules him out."

J.T. reached out and wiped his napkin at the corner of her mouth. "You had some juice there."

"Thanks," she murmured while her heartbeat kicked up a notch. The gesture suddenly made the atmosphere in the car intimate.

"You know when the case is over with we need to talk about this."

What? This intense attraction between us? These emotions that scare me, make me feel so vulnerable?
"Yes." She dropped her gaze away from his handsome face and concentrated on the pile of fries in the sack in her lap. She took one and nibbled on it. His presence so close to her sharpened her senses, all centered on him.

"I don't want to ignore what's happening here like we did last summer. You make me feel as though somehow everything will work out."

The huskiness that laced his words caused her pulse to beat even faster. She peered at him. "We will catch the kidnapper."

He smiled, a smile that encompassed his whole face, the kind that did funny things to her insides. "I know. I think we're close."

"Let's hope Paul had a productive trip this morning." Madison finished the last bite of her hamburger and patted her napkin along her mouth.

J.T. scrunched his trash into a ball and stuffed it into his paper sack, then straightened and started the engine. "Come on. I want to relieve Colin and Emma of watching Ashley and be there for Kim and Neil when they get home from school. We need to make the most of the next couple of hours."

"You're right. Let's go."

He backed out of the parking space, then directed his Jeep toward the station down the road. Two minutes later they entered.

"Boss, Agent Kendall just called." Derek checked his

notepad. "He said that Max Dillard worked for Goldie's Grill for several years. The owners changed once while he was there."

"Who were the owners?" J.T. stopped on the other side of the counter.

"Ann Laskey, then Cheryl Masters."

"Let's find out everything we can about those ladies."

"I've already got Rachel working on it. Kendall is now heading to Bakersville to check out another lead."

At the mention of the town where Susan Winn, aka Cora Baker, used to live Madison glanced around the large office. Susan wasn't there.

"Where's Susan?" J.T. asked, looking around, too.

"Remember, boss. She had a doctor's appointment in Central City this afternoon."

"Oh, yeah. I forgot she said something this morning about it." J.T. walked toward his office, pausing by Rachel's desk. "Come in and give me and Madison an update on anything you've found this morning."

"Don't have to come in. The only person I've been able to clear is Bobby Johnson. His alibi holds up. He doesn't have a girlfriend, or wife. He didn't have one when you put him away. He's an only child and his parents are dead."

"Okay. How about Timothy Connors and Aaron Adam Acker?"

"Still tracking some leads down. I haven't been able to find Aaron's sister or mother."

"Work on the owners of Goldie's Grill. Madison and I will work on the names on the list."

Rachel gathered up her sheets spread out on the

desk beside her. "I take it nothing panned out with Howard Wright."

J.T. shook his head. "We can cross him off, at least for Ashley's kidnapping. But when this is over, I will delve into his story about the porn and his brother-in-law."

Madison took the papers Rachel held out for them. "You've got great computer skills. Have you ever thought of working for the FBI?"

"Nope. I like it here."

J.T. continued toward his office. Madison followed him and took a seat across his desk.

"You never lived in a small town, did you?" J.T. lounged back in his chair, his fingers forming a steeple in front of him.

"No. Most of my life I've been in Chicago."

"Life here probably would seem dull to you."

"There hasn't been anything dull about Crystal Springs while I've been here."

A grin pushed through his serious expression. "That's unusual. Believe me, kidnapping and murder don't usually happen here."

"And you aren't bored?"

He laughed, but it was a humorless sound. "I worked in Chicago for years. My focus is different now. My family is the most important thing in my life. It took hitting rock bottom to see that. Crystal Springs is a great place to raise a family."

When he mentioned family a yearning planted itself in her heart. Would it be enough for her? She liked the excitement, the challenge of a complicated case—like doing a jigsaw puzzle with thousands of pieces. But going home to an empty apartment was getting lonely.

Day ten, 3:00 p.m.: Ashley found one hundred and twenty-seven hours ago

"That's good, Paul. I'll tell J.T." Madison disconnected her cell and pocketed it. When J.T. looked up at her, she smiled. "Paul just called. He's heading back here. Susan's story checked out. Her husband is one mean man who has quite a reputation in Bakersville."

J.T. breathed a sigh of relief. "I'm glad she got away from him. We'll have to make sure she stays unharmed. I don't want anyone else knowing about her other name or life."

"Paul was very careful."

He rose, rolled his shoulders and stretched. "I feel like that phone is glued to my ear at times. I need to get home and get ready for Neil's graduation. Ashley, Kim and I will pick you up—"

"Yes! I found a connection."

Madison whirled around at the sound of Rachel's shout and hurried into the main office. J.T. came up behind Madison. "What connection?"

Rachel jumped to her feet, grinning from ear to ear. "Ann Laskey was Chris Kline's mother. She married Bud Laskey and ran Goldie's Grill where Max Dillard worked."

"What happened to Ann Laskey? Where is she?" J.T. covered the space between him and Rachel and stared down at her computer screen.

In black letters he saw his answer. Cora Ann Kline

married Bud Laskey, then Ralph Baker. No! He blinked as though that would change what was on the monitor. He glanced toward Madison who was making her way toward him. "It's Susan."

"Susan? What do you mean?" Rachel asked from behind him.

Madison peered at the computer, sucking in a sharp breath. "She was so convincing yesterday."

"Because what she said was true."

"Boss, what are you talking about?"

He turned toward Rachel. "Cora Baker bought a false identity and disappeared. We know her as Susan Winn. Our screening for staff other than deputies only checks for a criminal record. It wouldn't catch an assumed name, purchased illegally." The thought that he'd been fooled made his anger boil. "She has to be the kidnapper. It's too much of a coincidence that she just happens to end up in Crystal Springs working for the man who put her son in prison, a son who died in prison three years ago."

"Do you remember Chris Kline's mother at the trial?" Madison asked.

He closed his eyes and tried to remember when he had last seen Kline. The woman he pictured in his mind was different from Susan—heavier, brown hair, large nose. "Can you pull up a picture of Cora Baker or Ann Laskey, Rachel?"

Rachel moved back to the computer and began typing. In a few minutes a photo popped up on the screen. "Driver's license from four years ago."

"Susan has altered her appearance, lost a lot of weight, but I can see a similarity around the eyes and mouth. Same height. Did she threaten you, J.T.?" Madison took out her cell.

"At the trial I remember she fell apart when the verdict was read, screaming hysterically. I didn't stay around. I was working another case and needed to meet my partner." J.T. withdrew his keys and started for the entrance. "Madison and I are going to her place. Put an APB out on Susan Winn, Rachel. Let the other deputies know we're looking for her and that she is considered armed and dangerous. Then get me a warrant for Susan's apartment and call Colin to let him know what's going on. Ask him to look out for my children."

While he made his way to his Jeep, Madison called Paul to let him know what was going on. J.T. pressed his foot on the accelerator, speeding toward the far side of Crystal Springs.

"Do you think she's at her place?" In the front seat Madison angled around toward him.

"Probably not, but we have to check. I know she doesn't have a basement, but my gut is telling me it's her."

"Then where did she keep Ashley?"

"Don't know." He came to a screeching halt in front of a two-story white brick building with four apartments. "Hers is the right one on the first floor. There's only one way into her place." He checked the driveway on the left side of the house. "Her car is gone."

"Is it a white one?"

"No, a black Honda. From the beginning we have been toyed with by someone who knows what's going on and has planned this for a long time." He thought back over the past week and all the times Susan was supportive and always there to help. She even signed in the volunteers who searched for Ashley. The irony of that struck him as though he had been punched in the stomach.

Inside he knocked on Susan's door. He waited a minute then pounded again. When no one answered, he tried the handle. It was locked. He started to slam his shoulder into the wooden door when Madison stayed his forward motion with a hand on his arm.

"Let's wait for the warrant. Rachel should be here shortly. We don't want Susan getting off because we didn't follow the rules. If she's in there, she can't get away. We'll block the only way out."

For the next ten minutes J.T. prowled the foyer of the building. His mind reeled with emotions he tried to suppress. This wasn't the time to explode with anger.

Lord, give me the strength to see this through to the end and not blow it. All I want to do right now is get my hands around Susan's neck and make her suffer like my daughter did—like my whole family.

"How could she take Ashley?" J.T. stopped in the middle of the hallway and faced Madison. "She's been over to my house for dinner before. She's come to my children's birthday parties. She…" Despite his resolve, fury welled in him and cut off his words.

Madison hurried to him and gripped his hands. "Don't think about that right now. She's had several years to fine-tune her plan. It's obvious she came to Crystal Springs two years ago to do harm to you and your family."

"I don't like what she makes me feel. I wish her husband had permanently taken care of her so that my family wouldn't have gone through this past week and a half. That's wrong, Madison, but I'm finding it hard to forgive."

"You wouldn't be human if you didn't have those feelings. Give yourself time. You're still processing her betrayal. This is a woman you counted on, cared about."

"And she used that." He gritted his teeth, his fingers tightening around Madison's.

She tilted the corners of her mouth up. "You know, both of us were right. This was an act of revenge connected to your old life in Chicago *and* it was a person close to you here in Crystal Springs."

"I would have preferred you being wrong."

"So would I," Madison murmured as the front door opened and Rachel rushed inside.

"I've got the warrant, boss." Rachel waved a piece of paper.

"Then let's break down this door."

"You don't have to." Rachel pulled out a lock pick from her back pocket. In a short time she had Susan's door unlocked.

"Interesting." J.T. pushed into the apartment and stopped a few feet inside.

Any personal touches that had been on Susan's tables were gone. He walked to the coat closet and saw that it was empty. Without a word he strode into the only bedroom and checked its closet and drawers. Nothing.

"She's gone," J.T. said to Rachel, who had come into the room with him.

"J.T.," Madison called. "You need to see this in the kitchen."

When he entered the small room with a table for two

in front of the window, he found Madison staring down at an open magazine on the counter. A pair of scissors lay next to it.

"She used this to make the note she left with Ashley." Madison pointed down at the paper before her.

J.T. came to her side and noticed a few red letters cut out and sprawled across the printed page. "She wanted me to know."

"Yeah."

"Another taunt."

"Her last one. We've got her, J.T. You've got an APB out on her. We'll find her."

"She's been gone for hours. She could be in the next state by now."

Madison took his hand. "Do you have a photo of her?"

"She never liked her picture being taken, but I think Neil got one at the end of the summer picnic we have every year. If so, it's back at the house."

"Good. Let's get it and, Rachel, get it out to everyone, especially the media."

Rachel shook her head. "I can't believe Susan is capable of this. She always seemed so sweet and caring."

"Yeah, right before she went in for the kill," J.T. muttered as he headed for the door. "I have to make it to Neil's graduation. Rachel, will you see if the state crime scene techs can come in and process this apartment?"

"Will do, boss. I'll follow you home and get Susan's photo, then go back to the station and get everything moving. I agree with Madison. We'll catch her. She isn't as clever as she thinks. After all, we found out who she really is."

J.T. hoped Madison and Rachel were right because it was his family that was in danger if they didn't find Susan. He didn't want to live wondering when she would reappear to make his life a living nightmare. This had to end.

Day eleven, 7:00 p.m.: Ashley found one hundred and thirty-one hours ago

J.T. sat in the high school auditorium with his two daughters and Madison next to him. He was surrounded by friends. His deputies were positioned in the crowd. Most of the fifty graduating seniors were seated in front of the stage, except a few who were participating in the program. His son was behind the stage waiting for commencement to begin.

J.T. peered at the podium. He had done everything he could in regards to Susan's apprehension. Now all he could do was wait.

Lord, it's in Your hands.

J.T. slipped his hand over Madison's and offered her a smile. Along with God, she'd been his anchor through this ordeal. When he'd needed help the most, the Lord had sent her.

"I don't think I've been to a graduation since I graduated. Was Neil excited when you spoke to him backstage?" Madison curled her fingers around his.

"Yep. It's not everyday you're the valedictorian and giving the welcoming address."

"I would be scared."

"You? I didn't think you were scared of much."

"Getting up in front of hundreds would frighten me."

"Me, too. I'd rather face down a bad guy with a gun. Well, maybe not that. But it isn't one of my favorite things."

Madison chuckled. "It's scary how similar we are."

He locked gazes with her. "Yes, it is." As though she was the other half of him, he thought. That realization should terrify him. It didn't. It comforted him that after his failed marriage, his heart wasn't dead.

On stage the high school principal approached the podium to begin the commencement ceremony.

Ashley tugged on his arm. "Daddy, when's Neil coming out?"

J.T. looked down at his program. "Soon. He's next."

When the principal made Neil's introduction, J.T. squeezed Madison's hand which he still held. His son's speech was uplifting and full of wisdom for an eighteen-year-old. He must have done something right to have raised a son like Neil.

Thank You, Lord.

After a long minute someone rushed out onto the stage and whispered something to the principal. Anxiety gripped J.T., and he bolted to his feet. His gut twisted into a huge knot.

The principal stepped to the mike. "Please, everyone remain seated. J.T., we need to see you behind the stage."

J.T. hastened toward the center aisle with Madison following. He paused in front of Colin. "Please keep Kim and Ashley safe."

"Don't worry. Nothing will happened to them."

J.T. hit the aisle and jogged toward the stage, his heart pounding so hard in his chest that each breath he took hurt.

When he reached the stage, he slipped behind the curtain and found the principal, worry in his eyes.

"We can't find Neil. We've looked all around. He isn't here. He was right here—" the principal pointed to the spot in front of him "—before I went on stage."

"He didn't go to the restroom?" J.T. asked even though he knew that Susan had somehow managed to slip through the security and nab Neil.

"No. We checked."

J.T. did his own search of the area behind the stage while Madison interviewed everyone participating in the program. Ten minutes later he had to acknowledge his son wasn't in the building. As he started back toward Madison, his cell phone rang. He answered it.

"I've got him and I'll make a trade. You for your son."

The hatred in Susan's voice blasted him. "How do I know you really have Neil."

"Let him tell you."

A few seconds passed, then, "Dad, I'm okay. I love—"

"I'm at Ted's house. Come alone or Neil won't walk away alive. You've got five minutes to get here or—"

The connection went dead.

Ted's? Why there? Those questions ran through his mind as he ran toward the exit, realizing the only way he could make it to Ted's in time was to speed. As he threw himself behind the wheel of his Jeep, he dialed Madison's cell. She picked up as he flew away from the high school.

"Susan has Neil at Ted's. I'm going there to make a trade. Keep everyone at a distance."

"But—"

"Don't come near. Do you hear me? She'll kill him."
He flipped his cell closed and ignored its ringing.

*Day eleven, 7:30 p.m.: Ashley found one hundred and
thirty-one and a half hours ago*

Madison pocketed her phone, frustrated but mostly
more scared than she'd ever been in her life. Susan was
going to kill J.T. and possibly Neil if she didn't do
something fast. She hurried to find one of the deputies
to get Ted's address. She thought she remembered from
the year before where it was, but she couldn't afford to
get it wrong. J.T.'s and Neil's lives depended on her.

*Day eleven, 7:30 p.m.: Ashley found one hundred and
thirty-one and a half hours ago*

J.T. leaped from his Jeep and raced up to Ted's house.
The front door stood open as though welcoming him inside. As he entered, Susan stood in the entrance to the
living room with a gun to his son's head, her hatred of
him now clearly visible in her expression.

"Put your gun on the table. Slow and easy."

Sweat broke out on J.T.'s forehead. "Will you let
Neil go?"

"When I'm ready."

Using his thumb and forefinger, J.T. carefully laid his
revolver on the entry hall table near him.

"Now the other one around your ankle."

He bent over and unsnapped the gun and placed it next

to the first one. "Let Neil go. This is between you and me. He had nothing to do with your son going to prison."

"But you did." She shoved Neil away. "Go outside and tell the deputies that I'll kill J.T. if they come near here."

When his son hesitated, J.T. clenched his jaw. "Go! Do as she says." He never took his gaze off Susan and didn't breathe until he heard the front screen bang close.

"Bolt that door. The rest of the house is locked up. I don't want anyone disturbing us. I've waited a long time for this."

After he followed her instructions, she motioned for him to go into the living room. The drapes were pulled, shutting out the world. Two lamps blazed, but there were shadows in the corners where the light didn't quite reach.

As he moved, he kept his attention trained on her, waiting for his chance to overpower her. He hadn't come this far to let her murder him. He had a family. He loved Madison. He had too much to live for without going down fighting. If need be, he would rush her and take his chances that she wasn't a good shot.

"Why are you doing this, Susan, or should I call you Ann or Cora?"

"I don't care what you call me. You took my son away from me. He was all I really had. I thought after I married Ralph things would be better, but he beat me. Then Chris died in prison in a fight. My world shattered all because of you."

Keep her talking. "Was Max Dillard your accomplice?"

She laughed, a hideous sound. "No way. He deserved to die. He was the one who introduced me to Ralph. Max didn't know what was really going on. He didn't even recognize me after I tracked him down. A friend I kept in touch with told me he moved to Central City. He just wanted the money I offered, no questions asked. He was dumber than dirt, but he knew how to drive a speedboat and Ross's was one fast boat."

"What do you think you're going to accomplish here? You'll never get away. By now the house is surrounded." He had to buy some time and come up with a way to disarm her.

Her face slashed into a ferocious expression as though she were a wild animal. She waved the gun and yelled, "Revenge. Your life for my son's."

Strangely as she declared her intentions, a calm descended over J.T. as if God stood in front of him shielding him from any danger. Madison's words came to mind: *You aren't alone. God is with you. I'm with you.*

Day eleven, 7:45 p.m.: Ashley found one hundred and thirty-one and three fourths hours ago

"Rachel, get me into Ted's kitchen and I'll do the rest." Madison held the penlight directed at the back door lock while the deputy worked on picking it. "Promise to teach me how to do this when we get out of this."

"Save J.T. and I'll do anything you want. You remember the layout of the house that Ted gave you over the phone."

Madison tapped her temple. "It's engraved on my mind. Neil thinks they will be in the living room where she was holding him."

"Got it." Rachel slowly turned the knob and inched the door open.

Day eleven, 7:45 p.m.: Ashley found one hundred and thirty-one and three fourths hours ago

"Sit down!" Susan's voice rose as she brandished the gun as if it were a sword.

"What now?" J.T. kept his tone level. He took a seat on the couch.

"My picture is plastered all over every TV station." Susan prowled behind the sofa across from him, her gaze darting to him every second or two. "By now Ralph knows what I look like and where I am. You know he once told me he would never let me go—at least not alive. My life is ruined thanks to you."

"It's not too late. You can turn yourself in, and Ralph won't be able to get to you."

"And go to jail for the rest of my life? No, sir. Besides, knowing Ralph, he'd find a way to get to me. No one leaves him."

"Then why did you come to Crystal Springs? Why didn't you just run away as far as you could get?"

She rounded on him, the gun leveled at his chest. "Because my son's death couldn't be for nothing. I had to make you pay. I planned my revenge for years, getting to know you and how to hurt you the most. I was going to kill Ashley and leave her body for you to find." Disgust entered her expression. "But I couldn't. Ralph always said I was weak and he's right. I wanted to kill Neil. I couldn't." She cocked the gun. "But I can kill you."

Day eleven, 7:50 p.m.: Ashley found one hundred and thirty-one and five sixths hours ago

Madison crept into the dining room from the kitchen. She heard Susan's threat and the sound of a gun cocking. Taking a deep, fortifying breath, she swung into the archway between the rooms and aimed her revolver at Susan, whose back was to her.

"FBI. Drop your gun."

J.T. pitched forward and to the side as Susan spun on her heel, directing her aim toward Madison. Madison pulled her trigger as the older woman squeezed off her shot. Madison dived to the left, and the bullet whizzed by her head while Susan crumpled to the floor.

J.T. pinned the woman down, wrenching the gun from her hand. Blood oozed from a shoulder wound.

"Madison! Are you okay?" He glanced around.

She came around the couch as the back and front doors burst open. "The cavalry has arrived."

"About time." J.T. grinned, relief evident in his gaze.

Susan groaned, her eyelids fluttered closed.

Madison heard J.T. whisper over Susan. "Lord, forgive this woman." Then he rose as Kirk and Derek hurried forward and took charge of the captive.

J.T. backed away and stood next to Madison observing Susan's apprehension. "Why Ted's house?"

"When I talked with Ted a while ago to find out the best way to get into his house undetected, he said she volunteered to water the plants and bring in the mail. He took her up on the offer and gave her a key."

"She had us all fooled." J.T. shook his head.

"And I think I know why she wanted this house." Madison took his hand and pulled him toward the kitchen.

In the room she pointed toward a door that led to Ted's basement. A doggy door was cut into the wood.

"That's new. That wasn't there before." J.T. inspected Susan's handiwork.

"I think she installed it right after Ted left on vacation." Madison gestured toward it. "Look. She didn't even bother to clean up all the sawdust. Obviously housecleaning isn't one of her strong points."

"No, planning kidnappings and murder are." He put his hand at the small of her back. "I have a graduation to go to. I hope it's not too late for Neil to get his diploma—and now he can give quite a speech."

Day twelve, 11:00 a.m.

Madison rapped on J.T.'s office door. *This is it. I can't stay around any longer.*

"Come in."

She entered as he hung up the phone and turned a brilliant smile on her. Her car was packed and now all she had to do was tell him goodbye. It wasn't going to be easy, she realized, basking under the power of his smile.

"That was Ross. Jill returned late last night. She stayed in a hotel in Chicago instead of going to her parents because she didn't want them to drill her. They've been up all night talking and working out their problems." J.T. relaxed back in his chair.

Since two days ago when they had apprehended Susan, Madison had seen a change in J.T. developing. He was more at ease. The stress, ever present since Ashley's kidnapping, was fading. He really looked rested for the first time. "I've finished my paperwork."

"Not one of the fun parts of our job."

She sat in the seat in front of his desk, needing the width of the wooden top to keep from throwing herself into his arms. The past two weeks had been a whirlwind, a roller coaster of emotions surrounding this case. But now it was time to move on.

"Paul left a few hours ago. I need to be going, too."

His smile faltered. J.T. leaned forward, resting his elbows on his desk. "So soon."

"Yeah, I'll need to report in tomorrow—I'm glad, with such good news."

"Can you believe the lengths Susan went to for revenge?"

"You and I have both seen a lot as law enforcement officers." They were dancing around the real issue. "The sad thing is that Max was pulled into her scheme and she killed him for it. She wanted no witnesses, not even Ross's dog."

"I can imagine her pleasure when we checked out every false lead—the vanilla scent, the footprints made using a weight belt so the person seemed heavier, Ted's white car, Eric Carlton."

"Where she's going there won't be much pleasure."

"I talked with Ralph Baker earlier this morning. She stole twenty-five thousand from him before leaving." J.T. pressed his fingertips together, his gaze fixed on her. "I have no sympathy for that man. Anyone who terrorizes a woman, even someone like Susan…" He shook his head.

"She learned from a master. He terrorized her, and she did it to you and your family." She couldn't stay any longer, talking as if this was just another day while her heart was breaking into hundreds of pieces. She rose. "I'd better be going. I stopped by earlier at your house and told your kids goodbye." The memory of that scene clogged her throat. After hugging each one of his children, she had walked away. Her arms had immediately felt empty.

He pushed to his feet. "They'll miss you."

How about you? The question was on the tip of her tongue, but she wouldn't ask it. Their time together had been unreal. Reality waited for her back in Chicago.

A one-bedroom apartment that really wasn't a home. The thought intruded, sharpening the pain. She started for the door.

He rounded his desk. "Madison?"

She stopped. "Yes." Only a foot from her, she wanted to wind her arms around him and never let go. But since Susan's capture he had retreated behind a professional facade as though they had never shared any kisses.

He inched forward. "I know I've told you before, but I wanted to say it again. I couldn't have done this without your help. You kept me focused. Thank you."

She didn't want his gratitude. She wanted his love. There, the thought was out. She loved him. But they had met under the wrong circumstances. "You're welcome. I was only doing my job." The hoarse thread to her voice spoke of her tightly reined emotions. She needed to get out of his office before she broke down in front of him.

"More than your job, and for that you'll always have my appreciation."

Appreciation. Tears crammed her throat. "Goodbye." Madison hurried from the office.

J.T. started after her but halted in his doorway. For the past day and a half he'd wrestled with his growing love for Madison. What did he have to offer her? He wouldn't move his family to Chicago. He couldn't. He was a recovering alcoholic who had come close to floundering during the case. She'd been wonderful and supportive, but he'd heard the pain in her voice when she had told him about her father. No, she was better off without him. He turned back into his office.

Day twelve, 11:30 a.m.

Pulling over to the side of the road, Madison swiped away the tears running down her cheeks. She should have told him how she felt. She thought he cared, but what if gratitude was what prompted the mind shattering kisses? No, it was best if she kept heading toward Chicago. She should put some distance between them. Then she could think more rationally.

Madison steered her car back onto the highway and headed away from Crystal Springs. She was doing the right thing. Then why did it feel so wrong?

Suddenly in the rearview mirror she saw flashing red lights and a Jeep—J.T.'s—speeding toward her. Was something wrong? She parked on the side of the road and climbed from her car as he came to a stop behind her.

He jumped from his Jeep and strode toward her, determination on his face. "You can't leave."

"Why? Did something else happen?"

"Yes." He halted in front of her, inches away. "You can't leave before I tell you how I feel about you. I owe you that much. I love you, Madison Spencer, and I want to see if we can make this relationship work."

The tears, lately so near the surface, flowed again from her eyes. "You love me?"

"Yes."

She did what she wanted to do in his office. She threw her arms around him, pressing her cheek against his chest, listening to the thudding of his heartbeat. "I love you, too."

He leaned back. "You do?"

She cradled his face. "Very much."

"This won't be easy. I can't move to Chicago. It's not a place I want to raise my family, too many memories best left in the past."

"And I would never ask you to."

"Then that means we'll be two hours away from each other."

"Yes, for the time being. But I can put in for a transfer to Central City's FBI office. A lot of people in Crystal Springs work in Central City."

"Are you sure? It's a small office compared to Chicago. Probably not nearly as exciting."

"I'm sure of one thing. I love you and I want to see if we can work it out. That won't happen if we live two hours away from each other."

He grinned and brought her closer. "I like your way of thinking. We make a good team." He framed her face with his hands and kissed her.

EPILOGUE

"I present to you, Mr. and Mrs. Logan," Colin announced in front of the altar of Faith Community Church, closing his Bible.

Madison turned in unison with J.T. and faced the crowded church. All were on their feet and clapping. Joy filled her. She'd found a home with a man she loved with all her heart. She'd found a family, a family that was healing from its ordeal. Her gaze swept from Neil, standing up for his father as best man, to Kim and Ashley, her maids of honor.

"Ready to greet our guests, Mrs. Logan?"

She smiled at her husband. "I don't think they are all going to fit into the rec hall. Half the town must be here."

J.T. took her hand and headed down the long center aisle. "What a way to end the year."

"And begin a new one tomorrow," Madison said over the loud applause following them as they made their way down the aisle and into their new life together.

Dear Reader,

Vanished was one of the hardest books I've written. The emotional trauma of a child being kidnapped would be one of the worst ordeals a parent would have to deal with. Putting myself in J.T.'s shoes was difficult. I felt I was going through his pain, as well. J.T.'s faith was what sustained him through the crisis.

In *Vanished,* J.T. faced his alcoholism all over again. He had conquered it years before and was a recovering alcoholic who hadn't taken a drink in almost six years. But when he was emotionally at his lowest, he was tempted to take a drink. It was Madison's reminding him of the power of the Lord that helped him to weather his need for alcohol. In the end the crisis strengthened him. A recovering alcoholic is just a drink away from being an active alcoholic. He or she needs a good support system, and J.T. had it with AA, his faith, friends and family.

I love hearing from readers. You can contact me at P.O. Box 2074, Tulsa, OK 74101, or visit my Web site at www.margaretdaley.com where you can sign up for my quarterly newsletter, sign my guest book or e-mail me.

Best wishes,

Margaret Daley

QUESTIONS FOR DISCUSSION

1. J. T. Logan faces his worst nightmare as a parent. How has your faith helped you to weather a crisis? Which Bible verses have given you strength through the crisis?

2. In the end J.T. forgives the kidnapper. Have you forgiven someone lately for a transgression that was particularly hard for you to forgive? How does your faith prepare you for that?

3. Guilt can consume us. J.T. lived with the guilt over his wife for years. How can guilt affect your life? How do you use your faith to help you work through your guilt?

4. Madison is afraid to risk falling in love again because she is hurt. Risk is part of life. When and how have you had to learn that? What risks are important enough to take? What risks should not be taken? Where do we draw the line?

5. Fear is a major theme in this story. J.T. faces the fear of losing one or more of his children. Ashley faces the fear of being a captive. Even Neil and Kim must face their fears concerning someone targeting their family. Proverbs 29:25 says, "The fear of man bringeth a snare: but whosoever putteth his trust in the Lord shall be safe." How does this verse help a person with his fear? Have you ever dealt with numbing fear? Has your faith helped? Did you turn to the Lord or away from Him?

6. In a moment of anger, Kim wishes she didn't have a sister. Then when Ashley is kidnapped, Kim feels her wish is the reason why. Have you ever thought or said something you regret later? How have you resolved your guilt over it?

7. Madison's brother was murdered by a gang shooting. As a teenager she decided to become an FBI agent and help others in a helpless situation. That was her dream. What is your dream? What steps have you taken or will take to achieve your dream? How has your faith helped you achieve your dream?

8. When J.T. faces the kidnapper, he feels God's presence and a peace descends even though a gun is pointed at him. Have you ever been in a situation that was difficult, but where you felt God with you and were able to handle it in a calm, peace-filled way? Have you been in a situation where you haven't and needed to feel that way? What was the difference between those situations? Were you at a different place in your faith journey?

9. One of the hardest things to do sometimes is to forgive yourself for something you've done—like J.T. with his wife's death or Kim with her wish. We are often harder on ourselves than on others. How can you help yourself to forgive something you've done? Why can forgiveness be so hard for a person?

10. J.T., while a police detective in Chicago, turned to alcohol to help him deal with the ugly side of life. He began to drink more and more until it nearly destroyed his family and life. Have you or a loved one dealt with an addiction of any kind? What has helped you to get through it? Did you turn away from the Lord or to Him for help?

REQUEST YOUR FREE BOOKS!
2 FREE RIVETING INSPIRATIONAL NOVELS PLUS 2 FREE MYSTERY GIFTS

Love Inspired®
SUSPENSE

YES! Please send me 2 FREE Love Inspired® Suspense novels and my 2 FREE mystery gifts. After receiving them, if I don't wish to receive any more books, I can return the shipping statement marked "cancel." If I don't cancel, I will receive 4 brand-new novels every month and be billed just $3.99 per book in the U.S. or $4.74 per book in Canada, plus 25¢ shipping and handling per book and applicable taxes, if any*. That's a savings of 20% off the cover price! I understand that accepting the 2 free books and gifts places me under no obligation to buy anything. I can always return a shipment and cancel at any time. Even if I never buy another book from Steeple Hill, the two free books and gifts are mine to keep forever.

123 IDN EL5H 323 IDN ELQH

Name	(PLEASE PRINT)	
Address		Apt. #
City	State/Prov.	Zip/Postal Code

Signature (if under 18, a parent or guardian must sign)

Order online at www.LoveInspiredSuspense.com

Or mail to Steeple Hill Reader Service™:
IN U.S.A.: P.O. Box 1867, Buffalo, NY 14240-1867
IN CANADA: P.O. Box 609, Fort Erie, Ontario L2A 5X3

Not valid to current Love Inspired Suspense subscribers.

Want to try two free books from another series?
Call 1-800-873-8635 or visit www.morefreebooks.com

* Terms and prices subject to change without notice. NY residents add applicable sales tax. Canadian residents will be charged applicable provincial taxes and GST. This offer is limited to one order per household. All orders subject to approval. Credit or debit balances in a customer's account(s) may be offset by any other outstanding balance owed by or to the customer. Please allow 4 to 6 weeks for delivery.

Your Privacy: Steeple Hill is committed to protecting your privacy. Our Privacy Policy is available online at www.eHarlequin.com or upon request from the Reader Service. From time to time we make our lists of customers available to reputable firms who may have a product or service of interest to you. If you would prefer we not share your name and address, please check here. ☐

LISUS07

GLO...
Coz...

An ... s
pre...
until a VW Bug appeared on her porch. No one took
her complaint seriously—except the handsome deputy police
chief.

WHERE TRUTH LIES by Lynn Bulock
The Secrets of Stoneley

Miranda Blanchard spent her life as a prisoner to her
debilitating panic attacks. But Pastor Gregory Brown became
a steadying force in her life as she and her sisters worked to
unravel the mysteries that plague their family.

SHADOW OF TURNING by Valerie Hansen

Her Ozark hometown had always been a safe haven for
Chancy Boyd. But now a series of crimes threatened her, and
a deadly tornado—her worst nightmare—was racing toward
the town. Only "storm chaser" Nate Collins could help her
face her deepest fears.

CAUGHT IN A BIND by Gayle Roper

People don't vanish into thin air. Yet that's what happened to
the husband of one of Merry Kramer's coworkers. And in his
place? A strange corpse. Could Merry's search for the scoop
spell doom for this spunky sleuth?